Revere Public Library
Revere, MA
Est. 1902
Revere Public Library
179 Beach Street
Revere, MA 02151
REVERE
A CITY 1915
A TOWN 1871
CHELSEA 1739
No. CHELSEA 1846

OUTBREAK

Center Point
Large Print

Also by Davis Bunn and available from Center Point Large Print:

Strait of Hormuz
The Patmos Deception
The Domino Effect
Miramar Bay
Firefly Cove
The Sign Painter
Moondust Lake

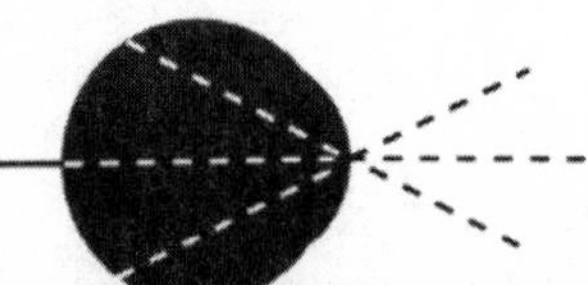

OUTBREAK

DAVIS BUNN

Center Point Large Print
Thorndike, Maine

This Center Point Large Print edition
is published in the year 2019 by arrangement with
Bethany House Publishers, a division of
Baker Publishing Group.

The text of this Large Print edition is unabridged.
In other aspects, this book may vary
from the original edition.
Printed in the United States of America
on permanent paper.
Set in 16-point Times New Roman type.

ISBN: 978-1-64358-222-1

Library of Congress Cataloging-in-Publication Data

Names: Bunn, T. Davis, 1952- author.
Title: Outbreak / Davis Bunn.
Description: Center Point Large Print edition. | Thorndike, Maine : Center Point Large Print, 2019.
Identifiers: LCCN 2019012617 | ISBN 9781643582221 (hardcover : alk. paper)
Subjects: LCSH: Large type books.
Classification: LCC PS3552.U4718 O98 2019b | DDC 813/.54—dc23
LC record available at https://lccn.loc.gov/2019012617

This book is dedicated to:

Dennis Brooke, Laurie Brooke, Mindy Peltier, Kathleen Freeman, Kim Vandel, Vanessa Brannan, Lynnette Bonner, Janette Lemme, Judy Bodmer, Karen Lynn Maher, Lesley McDaniel, Beverly Basile, Janalyn Voigt, Gigi Murfitt, Monique Muñoz, Gary Gilmore, Jessie McArthur, Ramona Furst, Janet Sketchley, Anitra Parmele, Mark Hall, Diana E. Savage, and Cara Dennis Thomas

And to the memory of:
Dave Jilson, Cornell Thomas, and Joy Gage

And most especially to:
Sarah Gunning Moser and Larry Moser

Steadfast.
Friends.

OUTBREAK

one

Avery Madison was awakened at eleven minutes past midnight by a most unexpected phone call.

The caller was someone Avery would never have anticipated speaking with. Not directly. Certainly not without an army of aides and lawyers. Just the same, Avery was woken up and ordered to leave his safe little Annapolis lab. And travel here.

The Atlantic coast of Africa.

Avery flew through the night and most of the next day, landed in Liberia, and transferred by chopper to a research vessel leased by Bishop Industries. Which was a total surprise to Avery, who took pride in knowing every aspect of his company's research program.

The skipper was a white Zambian named Trevor. No last name, as far as Avery knew. Trevor wore a stained uniform and a blond beard dappled with oily sweat. He showed neither surprise nor scorn over Avery's complete lack of knowledge regarding boats and the sea. Upon arrival, Avery went below, showered off the multiple flights, and slept for eleven hours. He woke at sunrise to a sea so flat and featureless, it looked like pounded tin. Trevor informed him they were seventeen kilometers off the coast of southern Senegal, approaching the Casamance River mouth. Before his midnight conversation with Kenneth Bishop, Avery would have guessed Casamance was a steak sauce.

Avery stood next to the ship's pilot and surveyed the empty vista stretching in every direction. If nowhere had a navel, it would be here.

Which was when the radar technician said, "Skipper, we've got a blip."

Avery's stomach had been doing swoop-and-dives ever since he'd boarded the research vessel. He stepped out onto the balcony rimming the pilothouse and gripped the painted metal railing. Avery could not see where the placid sea ended and the horizon began. His father the astronomer could tell him all the reasons why the equatorial sun seemed so much bigger. Just then, though, Avery was simply glad that the air helped to calm his nervous belly. There was no way he could be seasick. The floor of his lab was less stable. But telling himself his queasiness was all mental made no difference.

The skipper joined Avery on the balcony and said, "Time to suit up."

Kenneth Bishop's instructions had been brief in the extreme. The head of Bishop Industries had no idea whether his worries were valid. The World Health Organization had discounted the rumors as just another West African myth. Fears about health issues were regularly overblown, as Avery well knew. When Kenneth Bishop had made official inquiries, the WHO spokesperson claimed a poorly trained field nurse had spread unfounded rumors. Then the story had merely expanded with each telling, until the illness had become a shadow monster that felled thousands.

Only this time, the rumors ran in parallel with other secret reports Kenneth Bishop had received. The company's CEO had refused to give Avery any other details. He wanted Avery to go in, check things out, and report back. Without having his observations clouded by factors that may or may not be true. Which Bishop could not confirm. Yet.

Avery followed the skipper down the narrow stairway. "Where is it?"

"Nineteen kilometers and closing." Trevor opened the foredeck locker and pulled out a white hazmat suit and oxygen tanks in a matching white backpack.

"Is that really necessary?"

"You're the doc. But my orders were specific. You approach alone, you avoid any exposure. I bring you back healthy and in one piece." Trevor held his arms out. "It's your call. But if I were you, I'd suit up."

The heat rose steadily with the sun. Avery often worked in a bio-secure lab and was so comfortable with hazmat suits, he could type a report in his gloves or work with fragile lab glass, no problem. But struggling into the suit's stifling confines while on a drumming boat was different. The skipper had done this many times before, so he knew to start the battery-operated A/C and open the oxygen bottle's intake valve before sealing Avery's collar and taping the gloves at the wrists. The helmet came last, and instantly Avery was comforted both by the cool wash and the polarized faceplate.

By the time he was fitted and had inspected his equipment box one final time, the crew had lowered the dinghy into the water. The skipper performed a radio check, then Avery followed him along the lee railing, back to the stern stairs. Back to where the first mate had started the dinghy's outboard motor and stood ready to cast him off.

Avery wanted to be brave. He wanted to be as calm about all this as the boat's crew, but beyond that small craft stretched a whole universe of unknowns. Everything his safe little lab had kept him from ever needing to confront.

The skipper must have seen such geek-type nerves many times before, because he said, "We'll direct you by radar. We'll monitor you the whole way. Any sign of trouble, you say the word *alert*. Now, show me you're listening and repeat that word back to me."

"Alert." Avery did not recognize his own trembling voice.

"Good man." Trevor pointed to the second motorized craft now moored alongside the dinghy, then at the two crew members donning hazmat suits of their own. "You call out, and we'll be at your side in no time flat."

Avery accepted the first mate's hand and clambered into the dinghy. He stood gripping the wheel and watching the crew push him off. Out into the big unknown. Alone.

"The black lever is the throttle. It controls the engine's power." Trevor's calm tone came through Avery's earpiece. "Push it forward, slowly now. Good. Steer it just like you would a car."

Only now did Avery realize how thirsty he was. He licked dry lips and asked, "Where do I go?"

"Steer toward your two o'clock. No, the other direction." The man's voice did a great deal to help steady Avery's nerves. "Good. Now push the engine up a notch. Another. Okay, that's fast enough. Your target should become visible in about five minutes."

"Where will you be?"

"We've been ordered to hold well off. But we'll keep you in visual range from the top deck."

The moment of greatest fear happened when the sea changed. One moment it was all crystal blue. The next, the water became stained a sullen brown. Avery knew he had entered the Casamance River's runoff. Yet his brain told him he had entered a danger zone. And the glimmer on the horizon only heightened his dread, for closer to shore the ocean waters appeared to be stained a violent red. Avery tried to tell himself it was merely reflected sunlight. But his queasy gut said otherwise.

Trevor said, "Your target is fifteen hundred meters dead ahead."

"I see it." The fishing craft cut a low silhouette through the brooding waters.

"Okay, pull the engine control back a notch. Another. I have you clear in my binoculars. When you get close, swing the wheel to the left and slow further. That will plant you alongside—"

"Wait!" Avery said.

Trevor's voice held tension for the very first time. "What is it?"

"Don't bring the ship any closer!" Avery continued forward, then cut the engine when he was ten meters away from the fishing boat's side. He could see the barnacles, the wormholes, the stained waterline, the net still attached to the two cleats on the bow railing.

The hand.

"Avery!" Trevor said his name for the first time. Only he did not speak it. He barked. "Report!"

"Something's very wrong," Avery said. Strangely, the sight of that motionless hand dangling over the starboard rail actually calmed him. His heart raced, but it felt as though ice pumped through his veins. "I think everybody's dead."

By the time Avery photographed the three bodies and gathered blood and tissue samples, the skipper had suited up and joined his two crew members on the emergency boat. The inflatable was seventeen feet long and powered by another massive Mercury outboard. The crewmen drew the two craft together as the skipper climbed into Avery's dinghy. The inflatable held a pile of gear amidships, almost as tall as the seated men. The skipper asked, "You need more samples?"

The question confirmed the dread filling Avery's gut. "There are more boats?"

"Eighteen within radar range. None are moving."

"Then yes. I should—" He stopped speaking, because the skipper was already radioing for guidance from the mate handling the radar.

Trevor handled the boat with far greater speed than Avery could, which was good because the fishing vessels were spread out over a twenty-square-mile patch of water.

All of them were floating caskets.

After seven or eight boats, the revulsion diminished to a stain no stronger than the sea's brownish tint. Avery was able to look beyond the obvious and begin doing what he was here for.

Which was to search for reasons, and that meant analyzing the deathly scenes for similarities.

The problem was, he couldn't find anything.

None of the fishermen showed any marks. There were no pustules marring their skin. Nor was there visible evidence of a particular disease. The longer he and the skipper continued their silent journey, the more focused Avery became on the mystery.

All these victims had been cut down in the middle of just another day's work. Nets had been spread from most of the boats. The central holds were half filled with the day's catch. There clearly had been little to no warning. Which meant three things.

Whatever killed them had a very short gestation period.

The infection rate was almost one hundred percent.

The chance of survival was virtually nil.

By the time they had taken samples from the last boat, the sun was sinking into a blood-red sea. The Casamance River mouth was less than a kilometer west of them. When Avery closed his sample box, he asked, "Can we go have a look at the river mouth?"

In response, Trevor restarted the motor and aimed the craft toward the coast.

Fifteen minutes later they stopped and drifted a hundred meters off the southern shore. Trevor cut the engine and said, “That’s the town of Diembering straight ahead. Half the population fishes, the other half smuggles. In recent years, the town has spread to the river’s northern shore. The one bridge there directly in front of you is the only link other than boats.”

The beach was the same muddy brown color as the tidal wash. The vegetation beyond the town formed a green impenetrable wall. Avery said, “I don’t see any movement.”

“What’s more telling is smoke from cooking fires,” Trevor said.

Avery scouted the town. “What smoke?”

“Exactly.” Trevor started the engine. “We’re all done here.”

Only on the return journey did Avery understand what role the second craft played. The gathering dusk became illuminated by tiny flickering flames, bright as floating candles. A dozen or more, all of them burning fiercely.

two

The worst day of Theodore Bishop's life began with a walk down memory lane.

All Theo's worldly belongings were packed into boxes that almost filled his front room. He had left out his coffeepot but stowed his go-cup with the last box he had been packing the previous night. The one that contained the framed photographs from his office. Theo had been too exhausted to take in what they represented. Which was why he had dumped his last remaining coffee mug in with the pictures. Searching through the box made for a tough start to a very hard day.

On top lay a photograph taken at the summit of Mount St. Helens, the last climb he'd made with his late best friend. There they stood, their arms linked with seven other good buddies, all grinning with the confidence of guys who thought they would live forever. Beneath that picture was the one from his good-bye bash, when he stepped down from the city council. The surprise party was given by Asheville's mayor, which was good of her after Theo had refused point-blank to run for another term. And below that, the photo of his parents on their fortieth anniversary, just six months before his father passed away.

Theo was still holding that picture when the phone rang.

The caller ID showed another lawyer on the line. Theo and Harper, his best friend and business partner, had been dealing with attorneys almost constantly for five weeks and counting. He pulled the go-cup from the box and debated whether to answer. But since he was headed to court anyway, he decided it really didn't matter.

The man on the other end said, "My name is Preston Borders. I represent your brother, Kenneth."

The news was jarring enough to halt Theo in the process of filling his go-cup. "What's the matter with him?"

"Nothing, as far as I am aware."

"I haven't spoken with Kenny in four years."

"A fact your brother very much regrets." The attorney's voice held the rich baritone of a man who spent his days around power and money. "Mr. Bishop needs to speak with you."

"Tell him to call me next week."

"Unfortunately, that will not suffice. Your brother considers this of the utmost urgency—"

Theo cut the connection, filled his go-cup, and walked around the moving boxes. It felt as though he had become locked away in some legal prison, isolated from everything he held dear. Of course his brother would call. Through a lawyer. Today of all days. Of course.

Kenneth had called or written from time to time. Until four years ago. That particular conversation had been the week they laid their mother to rest. Theo had been aching from the loss. Kenny, however, had spoken as though the world had not shifted on its axis. Which was exactly how her passing felt to Theo. Instead, Kenny had started gloating over his latest acquisition. A yacht, a house, a business acquisition, something. At first, Theo could not actually believe what he was hearing. Kenny had bragged in his usual offhand manner. The winner displaying his latest prize. Only this time, Theo had hung up on him. And never accepted another of Kenny's calls after that. He had marked his brother's email as spam. It was easier that way. Theo had slept better as a result.

Which was why Theo filed the attorney's phone call away. Doing his best to forget an interruption he definitely did not need. Not then.

Theo was not someone who normally gave in to regret. He was by nature a man who found contentment in the day. But as he locked his front door and headed for his car, he could not help but wish that he and Harper had never gone into business for themselves. Until he'd been bitten by the start-up bug, Theo had been content with his life as a college professor. He was good at his job. He managed to make economics interesting. The student body had granted him the Best Professor Award five years straight.

But here it was, the second week of June, and he had only recently gotten around to grading the final exams. The academic dean had actually threatened Theo with loss of tenure. He had missed the last three required faculty meetings. He was late with two papers due for publication. He had not hiked in months. The entire spring had passed unnoticed. His life was a complete mess.

All for this. So he could drive downtown. And enter the city's main courthouse, and join his best friend, and wait their turn in front of the bankruptcy judge.

Theo was seated in the courthouse's third-floor corridor. The wooden bench was incredibly uncomfortable, but it was better than being inside the courtroom, where a couple wept their way through losing everything. Next to him sat Harper, his attorney and the ex-company's ex-vice-president. Harper was ten years older than Theo's thirty-seven.

Harper's mother was Hispanic, her father African American. Her skin was the shade of sourwood honey, and she balanced her strength with a gentle spirit. Harper's late husband, Grant, had been Theo's closest friend in the world. They had hiked, camped, trekked, climbed, and dreamed of taking on the trails of five continents. Then, four years ago, Grant had been felled by a heart attack.

No one had any idea he carried a congenital defect, not even their doctor, until Grant was gone.

"Know what I've been thinking?" Harper leaned her head against the painted concrete wall. The overhead fluorescents accentuated the tragic cast to her features. "Something a client once told me. Back when I was young and bulletproof. That bankruptcy feels like a small death."

Theo had no idea how to respond. Then he was saved from possibly saying the wrong thing by the ringing of his phone. He pulled it from his pocket, read the screen, and said, "Unbelievable."

"More bad news?"

"In a way." Theo rejected the call, sending it to voicemail. But Harper was watching him, so he said, "It's a woman I fell in love with once. We haven't spoken in years."

Harper clearly liked having something other than their troubles to focus on. "Why not?"

"My brother married her."

"You're making this up."

"He actually flew her away in his Gulfstream."

Harper's grin came slowly. Like she had to remember how to smile. "Why am I only hearing about this now?"

"What, you don't have any skeletons in your secret closet?"

"Fine. Forget I asked." When Theo's phone rang again, Harper said, "Is it her?"

"I don't believe this."

"Put it on speaker."

"No." Theo rejected the call again and pocketed the phone. "This is low even for Kenny."

Harper asked, "Your brother the billionaire is reaching out to you through his wife?"

"He tried using a lawyer this morning. That didn't work either." Theo liked giving Harper a reason to smile. So he added, "Officially, Kenny's holdings haven't crested the billion-dollar mark yet. *Fortune* magazine puts him at just over eight hundred and fifty million."

"From where I'm sitting, that's close enough."

Theo nodded. "I'm really sorry for bringing you down like this."

"For the record, none of it is your fault."

Her words helped, and so did her genuine concern. "You're a pal."

"And don't you forget it."

Their idea had been a good one. Great, in fact. Although Asheville was the commercial hub for all the eastern Appalachians, it remained underserved by most wholesale distributors. The reasons were clear enough. Travel was restricted to a couple of major thoroughfares. Companies located off the interstates were hard to get to and, in the winter, often cut off by bad weather. Most of the local companies were small and family-owned. Theo's idea had come from a conversation following a faculty meeting. A professor from the biology department had described how it was cheaper for his department to buy their equipment from Sam's Club rather than order it through the local wholesaler. So Theo and Harper started a regional distribution company to supply doctors' offices, labs, clinics, and small county hospitals. Their operation was to be partly owned by all the groups they supplied. If they profited, so did the locals. Simple.

It worked great for all of eighteen months. Then the largest regional distributors realized they were losing customers. Both came after Theo's group with paring knives—slashing prices, offering free transport, and doing everything they could to crush this new competition. They had deep pockets, while Theo's group did not. The big guys won.

When Theo's phone chimed with an incoming message, Harper's smile resurfaced. "Don't tell me."

Harper's grin reminded Theo of better days. "None other," he replied, and held the phone where she could read the text message.

She read the one-word message out loud, " 'Please'? That's it?"

Theo pocketed the phone again. "Apparently so."

"Please what?"

"Don't know, don't care."

Harper leaned back against the gray concrete. "What's her name?"

"Amelia."

"So. You and Amelia. She broke your heart. And it takes a visit to the commercial morgue for me to hear about it."

Having an almost-normal conversation with his best friend, here in this place, after all they'd been through over the past season, made it easy to say, "There was never a me-and-her. We met, she wowed me, she married the other guy, end of story."

"You never got over Ms. Amelia?"

"It's not like that at all."

"So why haven't you spoken with her before now?"

"Because of Kenny."

"Your brother the almost-billionaire."

"Right. Kenny and I haven't spoken for four years."

"Until his attorney called you this morning."

"Right."

Harper was fully engaged now. "What happened the last time you two spoke?"

"Long story. It was at our mother's funeral."

"So why now?"

"You'd have to ask Kenny. I won't."

Harper crossed her arms, a mischievous glint in her eyes, and music in her words now. "Am I finally learning why it is you're still single?"

"Of course not. Don't be silly. I almost got married to . . ."

Harper loved how he couldn't remember the woman's name. Just loved it. "Gloria."

"Right. Her."

"I never liked the woman."

"You mentioned that. Several times."

"Grant wanted to celebrate when she broke off your engagement and took that job in California. Fire up the grill, open a few bottles of champagne, invite the neighbors, the whole deal."

Theo recalled his best friend trying to be sympathetic over a woman he had detested. He was still trying to find a suitable reply when Harper said, "You're a good man, Theo Bishop. And you deserve better." Then her own phone chimed. Harper pulled it out, said, "The judge wants to see me. No, you stay where you are. I'll let you know when it's our turn before the firing squad."

Twenty awful, endless minutes passed before the courtroom door creaked open and Harper emerged. Her features were angled sharp as a living dagger. The last time Theo had seen her so riven by emotions had been at Grant's funeral. All the dread and resignation their conversation had managed to push away now came rushing back. Theo forced himself to his feet.

Harper said, "There have been developments. I don't know how to put this in a way that makes any sense." She took a long breath. "The case against our firm has been dismissed."

Theo was glad the bench was there to catch him. "What?"

"The judge and I just spoke with the attorneys representing the banks. As of nine-thirty this morning, all outstanding debts against us and our company have been repaid in full."

"How?"

"No idea. The bank's attorneys showed up with their scalpels sharpened." Harper turned as the courtroom door creaked open again. "Heads-up, here they come."

The four lawyers exiting the room populated Theo's worst nightmares. They passed the bench in a tight cluster, refusing to meet their gazes.

"Counselors," Harper said. When they ignored her, she watched them proceed down the hall and told Theo, "They've spent weeks preparing to carve our lives apart. Now look at them. Ain't it a crying shame?"

Crying was exactly what Theo felt like doing. "I don't understand."

"That makes two of us." Her voice had gone as shaky as Theo's hands. "Take a few days. We need to think carefully about how we should move forward. Those big boys out East aren't just going to tuck tail and walk away. Which means we need to work out a new set of tactics."

Theo leaned back against the wall. Breathed in and out. "This has to be Kenny's doing."

Harper stared at him. "From the way you described him, I figured Kenny would only cross the street if there were a dollar drifting down the sidewalk."

"That pretty much sums him up. The money to clear our debts, what were the terms?"

"I'm telling you, there were no strings attached."

"So maybe we just haven't heard what the real cost will be," Theo said. "You'll get back to your office and meet a new set of scalpels."

Harper's head was shaking before Theo finished speaking. "It doesn't work that way. It can't. The money came free and clear. Our financial records are completely clear. Our company is our company. *There was nothing to sign.*"

Theo had no idea what to say.

Harper went on, "Whoever cleared our debts can't turn around and say, 'No, wait, actually I want two pints of your blood.' The money was simply paid into our corporate accounts. Then the bankers informed their lawyers and the judge that our company is solvent again."

He looked at Harper and tried to form words, but they would not come. What he thought was, this couldn't have been his brother's work. It was simply impossible.

Then his phone chimed with another incoming message.

Theo's hands were so unsteady, he almost dropped the phone while pulling it from his pocket. The message was the same as before. One word.

Please.

three

While they were still seated there in the courthouse corridor, Theo called the Washington attorney and agreed to meet his brother at their family's former vacation home. Harper sat to Theo's right, talking with somebody in Washington, trying to get the lowdown on Kenny's smooth-talking attorney.

Theo's thoughts continued their jumbled meandering until Harper thanked someone, slipped her phone into her pocket, and said, "Preston Borders is a genuine mover and shaker. Senior partner at Borders and Blowfeld. Boutique firm, only eleven partners. K Street address, which is where Washington's power brokers plant their flags."

"That sounds like someone Kenny would hire." Theo studied his attorney and friend. Harper's eyes brimmed with tears and something more. Fear and hope in equal measure. Theo asked, "It's really over?"

"As far as the court is concerned, our new future starts now." Harper settled her shoulder against the wall. "Can you give me a handle on your brother? I've read the news articles. Some of them, anyway. When you and Grant used to talk about him, I would shiver, thinking how you could be related to somebody that, well . . ."

"Awful," Theo said. "A bloodless carnivore whose only interests were in beating everybody else to the next pot of gold."

"Strange way to describe our white knight."

Theo nodded slowly. "Something's going on. Either that or . . ."

"Tell me."

"What do you call that thing when a person's body is taken over by something else?"

"Spooky, is what."

Theo stared at the opposite wall. Kenny's image was so clear, his brother might as well have been standing there in the hall with them. "Kenny lives to win. He got his start buying defunct companies, picking them apart, selling what he could for a profit, and then moving on. At age twenty-five, Kenny was worth nine million dollars. His big break came two years later."

"The pharmaceutical company," Harper said. "I read about that."

"Kenny sank every penny he had into the acquisition. When he came home and bragged about his latest purchase, our parents urged him to walk away. 'Making money from other people's misery,' was how they put it. Kenny grew furious over how they refused to be taken in by his intensity and his drive and his sales pitch. The opioid epidemic wasn't even a thing then. But Kenny was there at the very start, and it made him rich."

Harper nodded. "I recall the press accusing him of being behind one of the companies feeding the drug mills."

"I saw that too. Kenny sold the group not long after that article came out. He made a fortune."

"Then he bought another company, right?"

"Yes. Vaccines and immunology. Cutting-edge research."

Harper stood. "Let's get out of here. I need to go breathe some free, clean air. Theo, you're coming to dinner tonight. And all you get to bring is an appetite."

four

Theo left Asheville and headed west by south. He spent most of the journey experimenting with the idea of freedom. Stretching his wings. Imagining a summer that might include something adventurous. Theo decided he would like that. Taking the sort of calculated high-octane risk he and Grant used to spend months planning.

Theo had not been on a major hike since the death of his best friend. He had joined other buddies on treks through familiar territory. But new and challenging journeys were easy to put off. There was work, and the city council, and invitations to speak at conferences, and a book, and so forth. Then he and Harper had started the business, and after that there just was not time. When disaster had started looking like a very real prospect, this was what Theo had regretted most. Letting life get in the way of his next adventure.

Theo left the interstate at the Fairview exit, something he had not done in several years. Fairview had once been a tiny farming hamlet. But that was before developers had reshaped two valleys, a lake, and the surrounding hills into the region's most exclusive development. Fairview Estates held three golf courses, two hundred homes, and a tennis stadium that hosted an annual pro tournament. The estates' wealth had transformed the neighboring town into a glitzy open-air market with cobblestone streets and shops from all over the globe. None of this had existed when Theo's parents had purchased their property, of course. His father had been a high school principal, while his mother had taught math at Charlotte Community College. They loved to hike and had come upon this land their first year of marriage. The nation had been recovering from a real-estate recession, and no one was interested in buying property this far off the beaten trail. Theo's parents had paid four and a half thousand dollars for thirty acres, most of which were too steep to build on.

Theo still cherished his memories of the cabin his parents had renovated and expanded. The original structure with its clay-chinked logs had served as his parents' bedroom. They loved to tell stories of those first years, spending summers without electricity or indoor plumbing. Theo's happiest memories had been shaped by his time here. But after his parents died, he had not visited the place in over a year. Then Kenny had offered far above the market value for Theo's share, and paid cash. Soon after, Theo heard his brother had torn down the cabin and was building a place that suited his monumental ego. Theo had not been back since.

Theo had never understood his older brother.

Growing up, Kenneth had been coldly indifferent toward him. They were seven years and an entire universe apart. Kenny's defining trait had been his competitiveness. Theo had never been frightened by his brother, but competition had always meant something entirely different to Kenny. Sports, scholastics, games—they were all fun to Theo. But even as a child, Theo sensed his brother had no idea what that word meant. *Fun*. Kenny's only pleasure came from winning. Nothing else seemed to matter.

The Washington lawyer had given him the access code to the main gates, which also shut off the home's security system. Theo decided to park his car on the road. His battered Jeep Cherokee did not belong on this property. He was the interloper here, the visitor on a temporary pass.

Nothing about the place was as Theo remembered. The estate was now surrounded by a fence of rough-cut granite topped by metal spears. Theo punched in the code and watched the massive double gates swing silently open. The long drive was shaped in a gradual S, so that the house remained discreetly blocked from view. The lane was fashioned of raked white stone that gleamed in the late-afternoon light.

The meadow of his childhood was gone. The entire thirty acres held a manicured precision. Not a blade of grass was out of place, nor a single bloom off its first blush. No leaf marred the emerald lawn.

The main house's first floor was granite and featured windows framed by huge redwood beams, as if it sought to copy the original log-cabin design. The upstairs was mostly glass set in more redwood pillars. The drive circled around to the left, where the hilltop had been carved back to permit two double-wide garage doors. Which meant the house probably sat on a windowless lower floor.

His mother would have positively loathed the place.

Theo settled on one of the veranda's wrought-iron chairs. From his perch he looked out over the tennis courts, pool, guesthouse, and the valley beyond. At least the peace was as Theo remembered. The summer light held him like his mother's favorite wrap, a glorious display of green and russet and gold. Theo assumed he would be waiting several hours but did not mind in the least. Making people wait was one of Kenny's defining traits. He took pride in manipulating others' schedules.

Then a helicopter started descending.

Theo checked his watch. Kenny was not due for another twenty minutes. His brother had never been early for anything.

The chopper landed on a concrete pad next to the tennis courts, blowing a storm of rose petals and dogwood blossoms across the lawn. The rear door slid open, and a pair of dark suits took positions on either side of the helicopter. Security. Theo watched them scan the empty property and realized his heart was racing.

Then his brother stepped out, waved the security personnel back into the chopper, and began striding toward Theo. One of the men protested loudly enough for his voice to carry over the chopper's wash. Kenny just kept walking.

Theo was shocked at the change in his brother's appearance. Of course, he had aged. Time stopped for no man, and over four years had passed since the last time Theo laid eyes on Kenneth Bishop. Even so, the difference was jarring. Kenny was forty-four now. He looked twenty years older than that. His expensive suit hung on a frame so gaunt that Kenny looked starved. His eyes had retreated into sleepless caves, and his cheekbones punched out so starkly they looked bruised.

"Hello, Theo. Thank you for coming."

"When was the last time you had a decent meal?"

"Yesterday, believe it or not. I just burn it off. My kids claim I've swallowed a tapeworm. How are you?"

"Fine. Thanks to your bailout, I'm doing well."

"You look it."

Four years had passed since their mother's

funeral, and now Kenny apparently wanted to have a normal conversation. For the first time ever. “Nice house.”

“Amelia hates it. She’s never been inside. I don’t—” His phone buzzed. Kenny lifted it from his jacket pocket, checked the screen, sighed, and stowed it away. “I’d like to talk. I owe you that and a lot more. But I learned on the way down that I’m due to speak before a Senate hearing in three and a half hours.”

Theo felt as though everything Kenneth said invited him to drop his shields. Which was like relaxing in the presence of a sleeping cobra. “Why am I here?”

“Right. We’ve got a lot of ground to cover.” The phone buzzed again. This time, Kenneth glanced at the screen and kept it in his hand. “I want you to have the house.”

“Wait, what?”

“Amelia insists she and the kids would be happier in town. She loves your place.”

Theo’s head spun. “You’re moving to Asheville?”

“Amelia and the kids arrive the day after tomorrow. I’ll come when I can. Look, I’d appreciate it if you’d make a trade—your place for mine. But that’s your . . .” The phone buzzed once more. Kenneth checked it and said, “I’m sorry, Theo. I really have to take this.”

Theo watched his brother step away, saw the

hand waving, the tense expression, the tight bursts of words. But even here the difference was evident. The cold rage that had always fueled Kenneth's competitiveness and lurked close to the surface . . .

Gone.

Kenneth ended the call, checked his watch, sighed, and walked back toward Theo. "Where were we?"

"I have no idea."

"The house. Right. It's yours, if you'll take it."

"Kenny, I can't. . . . No."

He nodded, clearly disappointed, but Theo had the impression Kenny had expected nothing less. "Can we at least trade homes for a few months? Amelia's folks sold their place before they moved into assisted living. I don't want her to feel pressured to buy, and it's important the kids settle in before school starts."

"Kenny, this place is worth a fortune."

"No one has called me Kenny in a long time. Amelia used to. Now I'm just the guy who's never home."

Theo had no idea why that would make his brother look wounded. The expression was as alien as this conversation. "That fence alone is worth more than my house. Which I would be in the process of losing if you hadn't bailed me out today."

Kenny's phone buzzed. He checked the screen,

then clenched the phone in both hands and spaced out his words like each one required its own punctuation. “You don’t owe me, Theo. Everything that follows is dependent upon you accepting that.”

Theo had no idea how to respond. He was still searching for the words when the helicopter’s rear door slid open again. “Your security detail are waving at you.”

“I’m sorry. We just learned that the hearing’s time changed.” Kenneth gestured to where the chopper’s blades were revving up. “I want your company to set up a new division that will contract with me to research a new vaccine.”

Theo felt all the old hackles rise. His brother had saved his company and now intended to rope him in. The risks were immense. Even so, one thing kept him from refusing point-blank.

His brother *never* apologized for *anything.* And yet here he was, saying he was sorry that an unscheduled Senate hearing was cramping his time frame. “Kenny, that doesn’t make sense. My group doesn’t have any experience in the field.”

“I’ll supply you with whatever you need, including the personnel. But that’s not the core issue here.” Kenneth started back toward the chopper, drawing Theo along with him. “You won’t understand what’s going on unless you take a trip. That’s why I came today. To ask if you’d go see what’s fueling my fears.”

Theo raised his voice to be heard over the chopper's whining drum. "Fueling your what?"

"I'm afraid, Theo. We could talk for hours and you wouldn't understand. There's a very tight window here. And you won't understand that either unless you see it for yourself. If you're going, you have to go *now*."

"What?"

"Drive home, pack, don't forget your passport. A limo will be there to take you to the airport." Kenneth was shouting now. The two security men were reaching out, impatient to draw him in and depart. "This chopper will fly me back to the Asheville airport. My jet's standing by. The chopper will remain at the Asheville airport and take you to Charlotte. You can just make their flight to London."

"You want me to go to England?"

"No. West Africa."

Theo froze in mid-stride.

"I know you don't have any reasons to trust me. But your only chance to understand is if you leave now. Will you go?"

Theo could not fashion a reply. His mind beat almost as frantically as the helicopter's rotors. His brother had just saved him from ruination. If Kenny thought this was so important, Theo probably owed it to him to go.

But that was not the real reason why Theo felt so drawn to the idea.

He had not been on any version of an adventure since Grant's death. Theo missed the thrill. Immensely. And now that he was free of the financial strains . . . Why not?

Theo nodded. "All right."

Kenneth responded with the day's greatest astonishment. He embraced his brother.

As he released Theo, he shouted, "I'm sending someone from my company to join you. Her name is Della Haverty, and she'll meet you at the London airport. Don't tell anyone else about this, Theo. Not until you're back. Secrecy is the only thing that will keep you alive."

five

Theo rushed home and started packing, driven by the memory of drumming rotors and his brother's gaunt face, watching him through the helicopter's side window. Theo could not deny the simple fact. Kenny's drive and hyper-focus were still there. But the bitter tension and cold rage had disappeared.

Theo stuffed clothes and passport and personal items into the backpack he used on longer treks. He decided to take time for a quick shower. He had not slept more than a few hours each night for weeks. His eyes felt grainy, and his shoulders ached for no good reason. He turned the water to as hot as he could stand, then let the spray beat on him until his skin felt raw. He dressed in khakis, a cotton shirt, hiking socks, and canvas boots.

The sound of a horn drew him to his bedroom window. A black Mercedes-Benz S700 was pulled up in front of the house, and a uniformed chauffeur stood by the driver's door. Theo shouldered his pack, threaded his way through the moving boxes, locked his front door, and started down the walk. Two of his neighbors stepped outside to see what was happening. They all knew of his ruined state and no doubt wondered what part a limo played in his bankruptcy. But now was not the time to explain. Theo waved to them, let the driver stow his pack, and insisted on sitting in the front passenger seat.

The driver was very skilled and the car very fast. They made it to Asheville's regional airport in record time. The driver stopped at the gate leading to the private terminal. Beyond the fence, Kenny's helicopter had already started revving up. The copilot rushed over and personally ushered Theo through security and across the tarmac. As soon as he was seated and the doors closed, the chopper rose into the air.

Once they were under way, the pilot came on the intercom, greeted Theo, assured him that using his phone was no problem, asked if he needed anything, and said their ETA into Charlotte was nineteen minutes. Theo waited for the light by the loudspeaker to go out, then phoned Harper.

She responded with, "You're in the man's helicopter? Like, right now?"

"Not just any old helicopter." Talking to her actually helped make it all feel more real. "This thing is outfitted like a yacht. Polished burl, doeskin seats, the works. How are you doing?"

"I've been tripping out ever since I got back from what was supposed to be the second worst day of my life."

Theo gave that the silence it deserved. He knew what she was thinking because he felt the same way. How much he wished Grant was there to share both the mystery and triumph.

Then Theo said, "Kenny just tried to give me his house."

"Run that by me again."

"He owns the property adjacent to Fairview. Thirty acres. Apparently his wife refuses to even set foot inside the place. They're moving to Asheville, and Kenny wants his family to stay in my house while Amelia finds them a new home. I need to ask if you can arrange for somebody to move the boxes out of my place. And for a cleaning service to go through the entire house. Tomorrow."

"This is for real? You're letting your nasty brother move the woman he stole from you into *your house?*"

"Okay, for one thing, he didn't steal anything. Amelia was in love with him before she ever met me. And you're forgetting the only reason I still *have* a house is because of Kenny."

"Good point. All right, I'll phone some friends. Tell me where we're moving your things."

"No, I don't want you—"

"Stop with your no's. Now, what's the address?"

Theo described the location and gave her the codes for Kenny's gate and house. He finished with, "I'll probably live in the pool house."

"The *pool* house?"

"Right. It's next to the tennis courts."

"The *tennis* courts." Harper laughed, a sound he had not heard in weeks. "Man, this is just too weird for Christmas."

The loudspeaker came on, and the pilot announced, "Sir, we're making our final descent into Charlotte. Please ensure your seat belt is fastened."

"So where are you headed?" Harper asked.

"Kenny asked me not to say."

"You've got to give me a hint. Like, is it an island northeast of New Jersey with eight million inhabitants? Like that."

Just saying the word caused Theo to shiver. "Africa."

The chopper landed at Charlotte Douglas Airport with less than twenty-five minutes before the flight left for London. An airline representative personally led Theo through the main terminal and past security, radioing ahead that they were coming. The hostess smiled as he boarded, offered to stow his backpack in the closet used by flight personnel, and ushered him into first class. Theo had never even flown business before.

His seat was positioned inside its own private alcove. The cubby was a treasure trove of miniature discoveries. The plane taxied and took off, and Theo dined on rack of lamb and fresh spring vegetables. As Theo ate, he reflected on how he wished he had someone to share it all with. He was rarely lonely. His life was full and his pleasures many. He loved the hills, the outdoors, the eager anticipation of another year of teaching. He loved academic conferences. He even found pleasure in writing articles. Starting his own business with Harper had been one of the greatest joys he had known for a very long time.

Those thoughts brought him back to the impossible day now ending. Beyond his first-class window, the sun set over a placid Atlantic. Theo knew he needed to work through all that had happened and come up with something that made at least a little sense. But the missing sleep that had built up over the past several weeks weighed heavily on his eyelids. The hostess must have noticed his state, for when she took away his tray, she asked if he would like her to prepare his bed. For a moment, Theo had no idea what she was talking about. Then she had him stand and used electronic controls to shift the seat upside down, revealing a mattress and duvet and pillow. Theo was asleep an instant after lying down.

Nine hours later, the hostess woke him as they entered final approach to Heathrow Airport.

six

Della Haverty watched Theo Bishop emerge from the first-class lounge's shower room and grew increasingly conflicted. It was a sentiment she had been feeling all too often lately, and she hated it.

She checked her watch, then decided it was late enough in Washington to call the *Post*'s newsroom. When her boss answered, she said, "It's Della."

"About time. It only took, what, nine texts?" Gerald Poitras made up for his total lack of journalistic experience with an aggressively nasty attitude. "Thank you not at all."

"I needed to check on something. And I've been in the air."

"Did I authorize travel?"

"No, Jerry. The company sent me."

"Where?"

She had already decided the less Jerry Poitras knew, the better. "London."

"No, Della. No. Your assignment is Bishop."

"He sent me."

Jerry snorted. "So you're getting close, and he shoots you off to Europe. Am I the only one who sees what's wrong with this picture?"

"His brother just showed up."

"Bishop has a brother?"

She watched Theo work his way down the breakfast buffet. "Dr. Theodore Bishop, age thirty-seven. Teaches economics at UNC Asheville."

"Same response. Get back here on the next flight."

"Before she left on maternity leave, Susan told me to follow whatever lead presented itself."

"But she's not here, is she? So now you're stuck with me. And vice versa."

"Jerry, I might be on the verge of a totally new story. One that—"

"Whatever you're about to say doesn't matter. At all." When she did not respond, Jerry's perpetual anger edged closer to the surface. "Nose to the grindstone, Haverty. Come back to Washington. Write up the assigned story. Or don't. Right now, I really don't care one way or the other."

"Jerry—"

"I've just about decided you don't understand the words *team player*." He hung up.

Della sat cradling the phone and watching the brother settle into a chair opposite her. She said softly, "Jerk."

Theo Bishop lifted his head. "Excuse me?"

She had no choice then, not really. After all, they were headed out together on this mystery trip to the back of beyond. So she rose to her feet, crossed the carpeted divide, and said, “You’re Theo Bishop.”

“Do I know you?”

“I work for your brother’s company. PR.” She offered her hand. “I’m Della Haverty.”

The swoop-and-dive Theo felt upon taking Della’s hand was as sudden and extreme as flying a glider through a downdraft. The woman did not fit any standard description of feminine beauty. Even when standing still, she emitted an electric rush so powerful, Theo felt his heart flutter from the charge.

Theo heard himself say, “Won’t you join me?”

She seemed reluctant to take the seat next to his but did so anyway. “I’m sorry you overheard that. I was talking to my temporary boss.”

He put her age at late twenties or early thirties. She was a few inches shorter than his six-foot-one. There was not an ounce of spare flesh to her lovely frame. He asked, “Temporary how?”

The question only heightened her discomfort. Her gaze was both smoky and blue, like a high-altitude sky seen through the early morning mist. “My boss is on maternity leave.” She bit down on what she was about to say next, and finished, “It’s complicated.”

Theo watched her gaze drift around the lounge, like she could not bring herself to look at this man who resembled Kenny Bishop. “I imagine that's a good word to describe a lot of what you must go through, working for my brother. Complicated."

She nodded slowly. "I never spoke directly with Kenneth Bishop until yesterday. He called me and said I needed to make this trip. Today."

"That sounds very familiar."

"Will you tell me what you know? I mean, about our being here."

"The simple answer is, I don't know anything." Theo related the previous day's events, starting with the call from Kenny's lawyer. That meant describing the absence of any relationship with his brother, which led to how much Kenny seemed to have changed.

At that point, Theo's natural reserve came rushing to the fore. He tried to stifle what had become more of a confession than a conversation. But the look in her eyes kept him going. Della Haverty's gaze remained locked on him throughout, scarcely blinking, her lips parted slightly. He finished with, "I couldn't tell Kenny no. Not even when he refused to tell me where I was headed. So here I am. A ton of questions and no answers. Zip. Nada."

Then he stopped. And waited. Wishing he could draw out the moment just a little longer. Truly sorry when she straightened, glanced away, took a long breath, and said, "They're calling our flight."

• • •

The journey to Accra, capital of Ghana, would take seven hours and ten minutes, almost as long as Della's journey from Washington. Della had no idea how she was going to sit next to Theo Bishop for that long and manage to avoid telling him the truth.

While the plane taxied, Della asked him a few questions, mostly to give herself more time to figure out what she should say. But when they reached cruising altitude and the flight steward came around with drinks, she was no closer to an answer. The longer she listened to him talk, the more certain she became that Theo Bishop was telling her the unvarnished truth.

Theo resembled his older brother somewhat, mostly in superficial ways. The differences were far stronger than the similarities. Della put Theo's height at six-foot-one, and his weight at rawbone lean. But where Kenneth was almost emaciated, Theo had the physique of a rugged outdoorsman. He shared a look of deep exhaustion with his brother, although in Theo's case the burdens did not seem to impact his calm. Or his looks. Which were, well, arresting.

Then she realized she had totally lost what he was saying, so she spoke the first thought that came to mind. "Why UNC Asheville?"

He tilted his head and smiled for the first time. The furrows lining his face rearranged themselves, and he became more handsome still. "You know I teach?"

"The brother of my boss, of course I know. Well, the boss of my boss's boss, to be completely accurate."

"The place, the region, the school's size, the students, they all suit me." He studied her a moment. "How well do you know my brother?"

"I've met him exactly once." She held up her hand. It was not a planned gesture. In fact, Della felt as though she was pleading when she said, "I don't know how much I can tell you. And if I start, I'm afraid I'll say too much."

"My brother told you not to speak with me?"

"Actually, I think your brother would approve of my telling you everything." She took a hard breath. "Like I said, it's all very complicated."

"Then let's un-complicate things. You tell me what you want, when you want. How's that?"

"Okay. Great, actually. You can live with that?"

"Yes. Just one question. Do you know anything about why Kenny saved my company? Or where we're going?"

"That's two questions." She smiled. "You call him Kenny?"

"Only because yesterday was the first time I've seen him in over four years."

"The answer is the same to both questions. No. I don't know anything."

"Well then." He nodded. "How about we solve

those mysteries first, then worry later about what you're ordered not to say?"

"I like that," she said with a smile. Della had always considered herself to have an excellent built-in lie detector. The needle had not quivered once in all the time Theo had talked. "I like that a lot."

Theo woke from a deep slumber when the pilot announced they would land in Accra in forty minutes. He rubbed his eyes and accepted the steward's offer of coffee. Della was still asleep, her face turned toward him and the sunset beyond their window. The golden glow suited her. She pouted slightly, as if struggling with a dream. Finally, he touched her shoulder and said, "Sorry to disturb you."

She straightened slowly. The smile she gave him seemed like a brief glimpse beneath her armor. "Are we there yet?"

"Soon." He offered his cup. "Share?"

"Oh, yes, please." She sipped, hummed, sipped again. Then smiled when the steward returned with a second cup. "What did I miss?"

"I have no idea. I just woke up myself."

Once on the ground, the plane powered toward the main building. And there it sat. Theo watched the world beyond his window descend into full darkness. The black was almost complete. If he leaned forward, he could see the modern Kotoka

Airport terminal. It glowed like a solitary lantern in a dark land.

Finally, Theo heard the aircraft's door open and felt the pressure shift. Almost instantly he smelled an incredible mix of odors, woodsmoke and spice and diesel and rank vegetation. He watched as a truck drove portable stairs up to the gangway. Then the steward returned to his aisle. He was no longer smiling. "Dr. Bishop, you are to come with me, sir."

"Can I ask why?"

"This way, please. You too, Ms. Haverty."

Theo found it mildly interesting how the crew and other passengers responded. The white faces watched their passage with weary curiosity. The Africans, however, refused to meet Theo's gaze. The steward handed Theo his backpack and stepped away as a uniformed soldier said, "Dr. Theodore Bishop?"

"Yes."

"Passport."

Theo handed it over. "Can I ask what this—?"

"Your passport too, Ms. Haverty." He accepted both, scrutinized them, and said, "Follow me."

"Will you please tell us—"

"You will follow me *now*."

They descended the stairs to find two more soldiers waiting on either side of the gangway. Beyond them idled a military truck with yet more soldiers. The officer walked over to where a white man stood by the truck and said, "They are all yours."

"Thank you, Colonel." The white man waited until the Ghanaian officer moved on, then asked, "This all your gear?"

"Yes. What's—?"

"Yours too, Ms. Haverty?"

"Tell us what is going on."

"My name is Bruno Seames. I'm head of your security detail." He gestured to the truck. "Climb in, please. We don't have much time."

Della dropped her pack to the tarmac. "I'm not going anywhere until I get some answers."

"That's entirely your choice, Ms. Haverty. But I and my men are leaving as of now. We have a very tight window to get you in, show you what's happening, and bring you out safely."

"Why do we need a security detail?"

"Come or not, that's all we have time for. Dr. Bishop, if you're coming, climb on board. Now."

Theo shrugged to Della, handed the man his pack, and climbed into the truck. The cab contained a rear seat that was little more than a padded bench. Theo's knees were almost in his chest. Bruno dumped Theo's pack in beside him and had started to climb into the passenger seat when Della said, "Wait."

Reluctantly she slipped in beside Theo. As the truck started to move away, she said, "I don't like this one bit."

The truck ground its gears and set off across the tarmac. The main terminal building passed to his right and then disappeared behind him. The truck followed a well-paved road that headed into the vast African darkness. All Theo could see ahead of them was the tiny mobile island where the headlights fell.

Ten minutes later, an odd-shaped structure cut a silhouette from the night. Theo became certain that up ahead loomed the biggest plane he had ever seen.

Then the plane's engines started. They growled a deep drumming note, one that grew increasingly loud the closer they drove. Theo was about to yell that they were going to collide with the aircraft when . . .

The truck accelerated.

And drove up a ramp.

Straight onto the plane.

The driver cut the engine, men attached ropes to tie down the truck, and Bruno Seames opened his door and yelled, *"Go! Go!"*

They sat there. Inside the truck.

As the plane taxied and took off.

Flying them into the African night.

seven

There was a light in a wire-mesh cage above the metal door leading to the pilot's cabin. When it flashed from red to green, Bruno's team instantly went to work. They released a set of tie-downs and pulled off canvas tarps, uncovering three massive clusters of equipment. As they began unpacking boxes and metal lockers, Theo remained where he was, seated in the back of the truck, because Bruno had not moved. Theo said, "Back to the lady's question. Why are we traveling with a security detail?"

"Here's what you need to understand." Bruno casually draped one elbow over the seat's back. His eyes were dark green and utterly blank. Theo thought it was like staring into a shadowed pool. Bruno was aged somewhere around Theo's mid-thirties, but his background had carved his expression into timeless lines. His years meant nothing. The quiet manner, the toneless voice, all of it was a mask. Theo knew this at gut level. Bruno went on, "My team does this for a living. We are very good at our job. Do you know why?"

Over the plane's thundering engines, Theo heard a slight accent. Dutch, perhaps. Or Afrikaans. "You're still alive."

Bruno's gaze tightened slightly, as close to

a smile of approval as the man could probably come. "We are contracted to take you into a very volatile region. From the moment we land, you do not use names. Not among yourselves, and not with us. There is every chance that others will be monitoring our communication."

He pointed through the truck's windshield to a massive black man whose tattooed arms extended from a sleeveless military shirt. "I'm Team Leader One, he's Team Leader Two. The others stay nameless because you will never speak to them. Anything you have to say, you say it to us. Tell me you understand."

Theo resisted the urge to respond with a demand for answers. He could see that Della was both tense and frightened. Arguing with the man responsible for keeping them alive, asking questions he probably would refuse to answer, would not help her state. He said, "Team Leader One, Team Leader Two."

Bruno's gaze tightened a second time. "Do you hunt?"

"Some." The truth was, Theo had never enjoyed it. He did it because many Carolina hill clans distrusted anyone who could not handle a gun or track a prey. So he had forced himself to learn both.

"Can you handle a side arm?"

"Yes." At least he could on a firing range.

"What about you, Ms. Haverty?"

"I . . . No."

"Okay. One more thing before I cover our destination." There was a subtle change to the man, a slight tensing to his features. The civilized veneer dropped away, and Theo looked into the face of a killer. "The situation on the ground could deteriorate very swiftly. If things go south, we survive by immediate extraction. If you hear me say *planeside,* you drop whatever you're doing and you run. If you hesitate, if you argue, if you think you need thirty seconds more for whatever you're doing, you die. Tell me you understand."

Theo heard the nervous quiver to his response. "Planeside."

Bruno opened the truck's door. "Time to introduce you to ground zero."

Bruno spread out the map on the equipment closest to the cockpit. The plane's lights were switched on now, giving the rear hold a harsh yellow cast. The map looked interesting. Theo had always had a thing about maps. This one was unlike any he had seen before. It unfolded from a packet hardly bigger than a wallet, but stretched out over a yard square. The material was silk or some other very light fabric, the colors so vivid they glowed.

"We are flying north by west," Bruno began. "We're staying well offshore because of two ground conflict zones we need to avoid. In about an hour and a half we turn due east and come in here." He pointed with an index finger on the map spread out in front of them.

Theo knew he should be frightened by all the unknowns. But just then he could scarcely contain his excitement. He was leaning over a cloth map while a highly experienced mercenary talked about *Africa*.

Bruno went on, "The southern provinces of Senegal are known as the Casamance Region. It's separated from northern Senegal by Gambia, which is this narrow strip of land stretching west to east. Senegal and Gambia are fighting over border disputes, so this southern section is isolated and highly unstable."

He pointed to a river mouth. "The Casamance River is the main transportation link between the coastal towns and the region's capital, Ziguinchor. Which means we're probably going to be able to make a clean, safe in and out."

Della spoke for the first time since entering the plane. "Safe from *what?*"

If Bruno noticed her strident fear, he gave no sign of it. "There are two possible sources of risk. The less important are the Jola tribesmen. They are the dominant force in Casamance, but they only make up four percent of Senegal's total population. The Wolof, the dominant Senegalese tribe, are the Jolas' ancestral enemies. The Jolas have been fighting a sporadic civil war for over thirty years. Yet virtually all of the recent conflicts have been farther inland."

Theo gave Della a chance to respond. When she remained silent, he asked, "And the greater risk?"

"The Senegalese Army, the region's only effective government. When this incident first arose, they tried to seal the area. But in the past thirty-six hours, fishermen and smugglers have brought out tales that all add up to the same thing."

Della's voice rose another octave. "And what precisely is that *thing?*"

Bruno refolded his map. "There is nothing I can say that will make it any clearer. Or prepare you for what you're about to see."

eight

An hour into the flight, two of Bruno's team heated up ready meals and passed them around. The food's smell mixed with those of the old plane and the adrenaline-stoked team, and made Della nauseous. She didn't want anybody to notice, so she took a plate when it was offered to her and pretended to eat. But Bruno saw beneath her façade and said, "We will get you in and out. It's our job. And there's nobody better."

Della admitted defeat and set her plate to one side.

The team continued to work while they ate. There was a swift coordination to their every move. They joked among themselves, the words spoken swift as bullets. Theo ate standing up, positioned by the truck's left fender, from which he watched everything. Finally, she walked over to join him. "Do you understand what they're saying?"

Theo smiled. "I don't need to."

It was wrong to like him like she did. Wrong to think she could trust the brother of Kenneth Bishop with anything, much less her safety. But she could not find a reason to keep herself from asking, "Why are you so calm?"

She half expected him to give a typical macho

response, as in, *It's a mask, I'm terrified,* something. Instead, he pointed with his chin to the massive dark-skinned warrior, Team Leader Two. "He reminds me of somebody. A hillsman named Clem. Not how he looks, but in the way he carries himself."

Theo turned and showed her the same open gaze that had so impacted her back in London. As though he did not know any way to be except honest. Which was totally absurd. Almost as crazy as the faint flutter she felt in her middle. Here in the back of the biggest plane she'd ever seen, flying toward a dangerous dawn. Ridiculous.

Theo went on, "When I turned fifteen, I took all my savings—three hundred and forty dollars—and bought this awful Ford pickup. The odometer had frozen at two hundred and sixty thousand miles. I spent a year rebuilding it. In the process I became friends with a local mechanic. When he spoke with other men from the lost valleys, Clem's accent was as hard to understand as those guys. They used their speech as a way of shutting me out. I was accepted, but only so far. I would always stay an outsider."

Della watched the team, saw how they excluded her and Theo, how this seemed to make them stronger. Tighter. She disliked it, yet there it was.

"Clem hauled my truck into the rear yard of his garage and basically guided me through the refit.

For my sixteenth birthday, he took me hunting. That next year he taught me how to track. He was the finest hillsman I ever met. I never much cared for the hunt, and he knew it. But he liked how I wanted to understand his world." Theo went quiet, then added, "Clem died ten years ago. I haven't thought about him in a while."

She licked dry lips. "Why are you telling me this?"

He pointed a second time at the crew. "I'm watching them, and I see Clem. The same steady nerve, the same competence. What you need to understand is, they will not let us down."

Della took a long breath, released it slowly, and felt the tight grip of her nerves begin to ease.

"You should eat something," Theo said, his eyes still on the crew. "Whatever it is up ahead that makes having a security detail necessary, you need to stay strong."

Half an hour later, the team began prepping hazmat suits. Theo's gut did a swoop-and-dive at the sight. Della stepped up beside him and cried, "Somebody has *got* to tell me what is going *on*."

One of the female team members glanced up and smirked. She said something, and the second female laughed softly. Otherwise no one paid Della any attention, until Bruno stepped over and pointed to the WHO initials printed on the chests. "The two white suits are yours. Bishop's company supplies the World Health Organization operations in West Africa. That's your cover. Our suits are blue with UN logos. United Nations troops oversee the southern Senegal conflict zones. If anybody other than Team Leader One and Two speaks to you, point to your IDs and say 'WHO'—just those initials. Don't say Bishop or your names. Keep your passport with you at all times. Your mic will be on the entire time you're suited up. The instant I hear your voices, rest assured I'll be on my way. So you wait. No matter what they say or how they threaten, you don't say anything more."

"But—"

"Hold that thought." Bruno handed them two plastic collars shaped like unfinished circles. "This is your wireless comm-link. Fit them around your necks." He showed them how his was positioned, with the earpiece dangling on a slender white cord. "The mic is located in the collar. Earpiece goes in your left ear." Bruno waited until the receivers were in place, then said, "Test, test."

"Loud and clear," Theo said. Della jerked an angry nod.

"Test your mics."

Theo said, "One, two."

Della said, "I'm still waiting."

When Bruno responded by walking away, Della's face went crimson. Theo turned back and said quietly, "Did it occur to you that he might be doing us a favor?"

"That doesn't make any sense."

"Hazmat suits," Theo said. "A thirty-year civil war. My brother buying me out of bankruptcy and flying me halfway around the world first class. Kenny pulling you away from whatever you were doing."

Della touched her lips with her tongue. But she did not speak.

"Something bad is down there. Something so terrible that telling us just won't work. Something *urgent*." Theo glanced around and found both team leaders watching them. Their expressions were very grave, almost furious in their intent. Like they were finally willing to show him their game face. Because he got it. "We'd better go suit up."

nine

Soon as they landed, the plane's tail section descended, and Della entered a blood-red dawn. She felt her entire body compressed by a feeling of intense claustrophobia. The helmet was a circular tent with a clear plastic shield that stretched from ear to ear. Her oxygen tank was encased in a white nylon backpack that also contained a battery-operated A/C unit. The tape sealing her white plastic gloves to her wrists felt overly tight. She could hear the others breathing through the small receiver in her left ear. In her other ear, Della heard the plane's massive propellers winding down. Smoke drifted in sullen clouds lit by the rising sun. She could smell nothing except the Windex used to clean her visor. The sense of being completely disconnected from the smoky terrain was disconcerting.

They gathered to one side of the open tail section while one of the crew eased the truck down the metal ramp. She and Theo stood at the center of the blue-suited security, all of whom faced outward.

Bruno searched the empty road and said, "Two, radio our contact. Tell him—"

"I see them, One," a woman said. "Your three o'clock."

Another team member asked, "One, do we off-load?"

"Hold on that."

An open-top Jeep careened down a rutted trail and halted before them. A tall figure in a white hazmat suit shouted, "Dr. Bishop?"

"Here."

"Avery Madison. Microbiologist." His voice sounded muffled through the plastic helmets.

"Set your comm-link to channel seven," Bruno ordered.

"Oh. Right. Sorry. I should have already . . ." He fumbled with a device at his belt, then Della heard him through her earpiece, "How's that?"

"Five by five. Do we off-load your supplies?"

The man's nervousness resonated inside Della's head. "I don't know."

"What's happened?"

"The army showed up about an hour and a half ago." Della could see his larynx bob through the face shield. "They started burning the village on this side of the river."

Bruno turned and stared at where smoke rose in great dark clouds, marring the sunrise. "How is it across the bridge?"

"Clear for now. But—"

"Where's your lab?"

He pointed toward the sunrise. "The white tent over there. See the roof?"

"How many in your crew?"

"Two plus myself."

"Radio the others. Tell them to drop everything and gather planeside."

"Our work has reached a critical phase!"

"If they stay, they die." Bruno pointed at the idling truck. "We take off in thirty minutes. They need to understand, we're the last flight out of Dodge."

The bridge was a single-lane steel structure from a far-distant era. Theo listened to the planks rattle beneath their truck as they eased slowly forward. He and Della sat in the rear hold, positioned across from each other. The canvas tarp had been pulled back, and the sky overhead was stained by cinders and drifting smoke. Theo's plastic facepiece granted him a one-hundred-eighty-degree view, but he still found it constricting. Finally, he rose and positioned himself by the central stanchion, a curved steel bar over which the rear tarp would be stretched. It offered him a stable platform as he searched in every direction.

The river was a sullen brown stain beneath them, perhaps two hundred meters wide. Both banks held villages with ramshackle houses crammed along the waterfront. Most structures were built on rickety stilts and descended toward the water in stair-like stages. Boats of every make and design crowded the muddy shore. At several places along both banks, oil rigs stood like silently rusting birds. Only one was still pumping. Theo also spotted four old-fashioned drilling platforms. Pipes and equipment lay scattered in the muddy undergrowth.

Behind them, soldiers stood along the riverfront and observed their progress. A pair of bulldozers worked in tandem, pushing mounds of dirt toward a space at the center of the village. Theo heard a hushed metallic roar and saw flames shoot up from several points. A man carrying a bullhorn emerged from between two houses and glared in their direction.

Ahead of them, on the river's opposite bank, there was no movement whatsoever.

Avery pointed back to where soldiers approached a white-roofed canvas structure. "Can't you do anything to protect my work?"

"You know the answer to that." Bruno was seated by the tailgate, a semiautomatic rifle pointed down at his feet. Team Leader Two rode in the cab's passenger seat.

Theo asked the scientist, "How long have you been here?"

"I arrived two days ago." Avery's voice shook slightly. Theo thought the man looked beyond exhausted. "No, three. The others landed yesterday."

Della's former anger was gone now. "What is going on here?"

"Plague," Theo guessed. "That's it, isn't it?"

"I wish it were that simple." Avery tried to wipe his face, then jerked his gloved hand away from the plastic visor. "Last week I was working at our main Baltimore lab when a friend with the WHO sent me an alert about rumors trickling out of West Africa. How an unknown disease had possibly struck several places along the West African coast. No one was certain of anything, so this alert came through unofficial channels. In our line of work, reports like this arrive from time to time. Usually involving a region that's impossible to reach. I filed a summary note, standard ops when something surfaces. Only that night I was woken up by my company's CEO, who ordered me to drop everything and travel here."

Della muttered, "This is making no sense at all."

"I didn't have time to apply for a visa," Avery went on. "Which turns out to be a good thing, if those soldiers are any indication of the official welcome I might have received. My company arranged for a research vessel to bring me north. And we found the fishing boats. Nineteen in all. Just floating in the Atlantic. Everybody on board was dead."

Della asked, "How many survivors?"

"None. Not in the boats, not here in these two villages. Humans and animals alike." Avery tried to wipe his face a second time. "No one has seen anything like this. The infection rate is total. The survival rate is nil."

"What killed them?"

Avery pointed ahead of them. "This side of the river, it was chest infections mostly."

"You're saying they died of a cold?"

"Or flu. Right." Avery pointed back to where the soldier with a bullhorn still watched them. "Back there it was the measles."

The news silenced the truck. They drove down one rutted track after another. Most of the shacks they passed were tin-roofed with wide front verandas holding flat pallets on concrete blocks, wide enough for entire families to sprawl or sleep. Cooking stoves were oil barrels with segments cut out so that fires could be stoked by people who were no longer there. They passed a side yard with an empty animal pen and chicken coop. A single shoe at the base of the steps leading into a house. A headdress trampled into the earth.

A bird flew overhead.

"Stop the truck!" Avery scrambled down before the vehicle had braked to a halt. Bruno signaled, and one of his team followed, weapon at the ready. Avery spun in a slow circle, his face craned upward as he watched the bird fly away. "What's the time?"

Bruno pulled out his communicator, checked the face. "Three thirty-seven local." Once the bird had vanished into the waving heat, he said, "Let's move."

Avery reluctantly allowed the soldier to turn him around and help him back into the truck. "Assuming the disease was airborne, we now have concrete evidence of closure."

Theo said, "You're not talking about the cold. Or measles. Are you?"

"Of course not." Avery continued to search the sky overhead. "We're thinking a cross-species virus that eliminates the immune system of any host organization it invades. Whatever illness arrives next is fatal. One of our first subjects was an otherwise healthy male, late twenties or early thirties, felled by septicemia. The only wound we could find was a fish spine in his thumb."

"Where are you taking us?" Della asked.

Bruno said, "The beach."

"To control the spread of any disease, we must first identify the carrier. How it spreads. Up ahead is the only possible answer I've uncovered so far." Avery pointed upward. "Another bird. That's good. Very good. Means the disease's life cycle outside a host might be limited to a few days at most."

"What I don't understand is my brother's involvement in this," Theo said.

"Who is your brother?"

"No names," Bruno said.

Theo replied, "Your boss, the man who called you."

Avery turned his entire body and stared at Theo.

"I agree," Della said. "Another killer bug erupts in Africa. Why is he so worried?"

Avery nodded. "He hasn't said. But I can guess."

"Do. Please."

"Not now," Bruno said. "We check this out, we hurry back to the plane, we get out safely. Then we guess."

The road left the town and passed through a strip of dusty wasteland. A few stumpy palmettos dotted the landscape. Three hundred meters later, they arrived at the beach. There by the river mouth the shore was colored a pale gray. Far in the distance the vista became idyllic, with shimmering gold sand and crystal blue waters. Tall imperial palms formed a living canopy that framed the beach. A few shacks had been built of driftwood and palm fronds.

"Here." Avery pointed ahead and to his left, where the river joined with the Atlantic. "This is what I wanted you to see."

Hundreds of drying racks built of driftwood and rusting metal lined the area where the road emerged from the brush. Beyond them lay dozens of ancient fishing vessels, mostly wood, but a few of stained fiberglass and even a couple of flat-bottom steel landing craft. But what gripped Theo's attention were the racks. Instead of holding fishing nets or lines of fish, row after row supported clumps of black vegetation. “What are they drying?”

“A species of seaweed. We’ve taken samples. Lots of them.”

“Why are they drying it?”

“Exactly.” Avery’s nod rocked his entire upper body. “There’s only one explanation for so many racks holding seaweed. They’re eating it.”

“Is that normal?”

“Absolutely not. Most varieties of seaweed indigenous to Africa’s Atlantic coast contain chemicals that are noxious to the human system. It won’t kill you, but it will certainly make you ill. There is no record of any southern Senegalese tribe eating seaweed except in periods of extreme famine.”

Bruno cut in with, “We need to be heading back.”

Avery might as well not have heard him. The scientist was in his element now. “Pollution and overfishing have seriously depleted local catches. So it’s natural they would go after any available source of either vitamins or protein. And this new variety of seaweed shows a remarkably high content of both.” He pointed to the shadows cast by palm trees lining the beach. “Over there, see those clay mounds?”

Theo studied the small conical structures. “They look like baking ovens.”

"Which is precisely what they are. The town behind us and the one on the opposite bank are built mostly with bricks made from river mud and fired in these kilns. Only now they all contain bricks of seaweed."

Theo struggled to construct a logical chain from what he was hearing. "So they are baking seaweed like bread and selling it to other towns?"

"All up and down the coast, and inland via the river." Avery held up a blue-gloved hand, stopping Theo's next comment. "Nowhere else around here has reported any such illnesses."

"You're sure?"

"We've checked as much as we could. Communications are—"

Avery's response was cut short by a low *carrumph,* a sound Theo felt as much in his chest as actually heard.

From the river's other side, a column of smoke rose lazily into the sky. Theo thought it was located close to the white-roofed lab. Only he couldn't see the lab now to be certain.

Then the air was punctured by the staccato beats of machine guns. Silence. Then gunfire again.

Bruno's voice was as sharp as the gunfire. *"Back to the plane! Now!"*

ten

They sped back down the rutted road. The truck's engine raced as the driver held to a bone-jarring pace. Theo and Avery and Della kept two-fisted grips on the railings intended to hold the canvas cover in place. The road was lined with dusty palms and head-high shrubbery. Through a cut in the growth, Theo thought he saw a second plume of smoke rising from the other town. Or the lab.

A new laconic voice clicked into Theo's earpiece. "One, this is Pilot."

"Go, Pilot. This is One."

The voice was smooth, calm. The sound of hammering metal could be heard in the background. "We're taking fire."

Then Team Leader Two's voice came through Theo's earpiece, "One, the bridge is blocked."

Theo rose with Bruno and almost bounced out of the truck. He saw a tank had pulled forward until its front end filled the bridge's far side. Its turret aimed at whatever might dare to cross.

Bruno's voice remained as calm as the pilot's, like two bored men discussing the weather. "Pilot, are all lab crew loaded?"

"Roger that. Hang on." A pause, then, "One, we have three trucks of militia headed our way."

"This is One. You are cleared for takeoff."

"You sure about that, One? I hate to leave a mate behind."

"That is an order, Pilot. Go now."

"Roger that. Good hunting, One. Pilot out."

Bruno's voice showed no concern whatsoever as he ordered, "Back to the beach."

Della heard Avery protest, "You can't be serious!"

Avery Madison's words shuddered from the truck's jouncing ride. Up ahead, the green opened where the jungle met the shore. The brilliant sunlight reflected off the sweat misting Avery's visor.

Bruno asked, "The craft that brought you and your crew are still on the beach, correct?"

"Sure, but they're just a dinghy and an inflatable!"

"That should be enough to hold us," Bruno replied. "Where are they stored?"

"A lean-to we found empty . . . I don't even know if they've got gas."

"Everybody keep an eye out for fuel canisters." They exploded into the clearing, and the truck rammed down a sandy track laid out by fishermen. "Where are your boats, Avery?"

He rose slightly from the bench. "Down on the left. But where can we go with them?"

Theo said, "Looks like there are fuel canisters stored under the netting up by the tree line."

To Della, Theo's voice sounded almost as calm as Bruno. She wondered if it was a lie, or if he really wasn't captured by the fear she and Avery clearly felt. "Good eyes. Two, take your team. Go."

The huge man and three others dropped from the truck. If they felt clumsy inside the hazmat suits, they did not show it.

The truck continued to lumber down the rutted trail. They passed several dozen drying frames, all of them covered in the same black goop. Theo asked, "Where are the fish?"

"They probably landed what came easiest, like the scientist said," Bruno replied. "What sold, and what fed their families."

Theo said, "There has to be a connection between the seaweed and this illness."

Bruno nodded. "Makes sense to me."

Della could scarcely take in the way these two men spoke, as if the hammering, booming noise behind them were only a thunderstorm.

The plane zoomed overhead. One wing trailed smoke. "One, this is Pilot."

"Go, Pilot."

"We're airborne, one minor injury, looks like shrapnel. Be advised, militia are crossing the bridge in force."

"Roger that. One out."

Theo asked, "Is that an engine on fire?"

"He's got three left," Bruno said. "Those

Constellations can fly on two, no problem. One will keep it airborne in a pinch."

Theo leaped down before the truck stopped rolling. When she tried to rise, Della discovered her legs were not obeying her mental commands. Theo actually seemed to expect it. He was there waiting for her with his arms outstretched. "Easy does it."

She wanted to say something nice, make light of a terrible moment, show she was as in control as he evidently was. But Theo had already turned away to help Avery clamber down. The man almost fell off the back, then frantically waved off Theo's help. "You don't understand! There's no ship! The research vessel left to handle another contract! There's no place for us. . . ."

Avery stopped yelling, because Bruno walked up and mashed his own faceplate against Avery's. "What would you prefer? Stay here and spend a few months being interrogated in the Ziguinchor prison?"

"What? No . . . I . . ."

"I've been there. Once. I'll tell you straight up: I never want to go back." Bruno turned away, the discussion over. "Let's get these craft in the water."

Theo helped Bruno's crew haul the inflatable down to the shore. Two's group arrived carrying fuel canisters. Together they dragged the heavier dinghy into the water, then loaded the canisters.

Bruno said, "Remind me to thank the next fisherman I meet."

When the two boats were in waist-deep water, Bruno directed most of his team into the inflatable and placed his second team leader and two others with Theo, Della, and Avery in the dinghy. Theo thought it was the right move. The dinghy was more stable, though it was also far slower. Which meant most of the shooters were situated in the faster vessel. Bruno allowed the dinghy to set the pace. The waves were small and feeble and slapped like little hands at the vessel's sides as they motored away from the beach.

Team Leader Two handled the dinghy's engine. "One, we have boots on the shore."

"I see them. Can you push that dinghy any faster?"

"We're topped out."

"Understood." Bruno steered the inflatable over to the left of the dinghy. "Get ready to return fire."

When Theo looked back, the westering sun glinted off weapons. A lot of them. The troops were dressed in bits and pieces of jungle fatigues, mostly green sweat-stained T-shirts and bush pants. The sun was setting directly behind Theo, which made the soldiers stand out in stark relief. As they lifted their weapons to their shoulders, the gun barrels looked close enough to touch. A man slightly removed from the others yelled something and fired a handgun in their direction.

"Rapid-fire," Bruno said, calm as ever. "Fire at will."

The nine-person crew let loose. The sound of automatic fire hammered at Theo. He unholstered his pistol and shot with the others, yet he doubted he damaged anything except maybe a few palm fronds. His hands were shaking too badly to take proper aim.

The soldiers scattered, some flattening themselves into the mud while others dashed for the palms. The officer's voice rose to a falsetto shriek. The shore became lit by brilliant flashes that would have been lovely to watch had the bullets not been aimed at them.

The boats continued to pull away. Finally, Bruno said, "Cease firing." Theo could still see occasional flashes from the shoreline, but then they too gradually stopped. Bruno asked, "Anyone hit?"

The massive second team leader left the tiller long enough to step to each person, touch them lightly, and inspect them through the faceplate. "We're good here, One."

As they powered into the setting sun, Avery fretted, "I don't see anything whatsoever good about this situation. We're sitting ducks out here."

Neither Bruno nor his second-in-command saw any need to respond.

"What happens when they bring out a boat of their own?" Avery's volume gradually rose. "Or a helicopter? What happens then?"

The team leader handling their outboard chuckled. "Then we die, little man."

"That's enough, Two."

"We die quickly, no problem."

"Two. Enough."

The man kept chuckling but said no more. Avery's shudders were visible through the hazmat suit.

Theo realized his breath was coming in tight gasps. "One, I'm getting low on air."

In response, Bruno released the shoulder catches and pulled off his helmet. He sat there for a time, breathing the evening air. At last he said, "All right, everybody, it's safe to remove your gear."

The dinghy had three benches that ran from gunnel to gunnel, and a fourth fit snugly into the bow. One of the armed crew sat there and faced toward the rear, scouting the sea behind them. Their crew's leader shared the rear bench with the smallest of his team. The air felt very good on Della's skin. The salty breeze tasted wonderful. Every breath carried the faint promise of life. No one spoke for a time as they motored away. The shore became a faint green shadow on the eastern horizon. Della couldn't see the soldiers anymore, but she had to assume they were still around, and that Avery's fears were very real. Even so, logic could not disturb the simple pleasure of being alive.

Avery, however, remained agitated and fearful. "Why were they shooting at us?"

When no one spoke, Theo offered, "My guess is, we represent a different version of events."

Della had been thinking the same thing. Still, Avery demanded, "What do they want to claim happened?"

Team Leader Two shrugged his broad shoulders. "Senegal is putting on a happy face these days. They pretend to the world that the south is under control. They want to bring in tourist dollars."

They all still wore earpieces with mics clipped to their collars. Della heard Bruno say, "They may just want to avoid giving the Jola tribe another reason to revolt. All this might simply be their way of sweeping bad news under the carpet."

The sun melted slowly into the water. Della had seen her share of beautiful sunsets, but none had affected her like this one. Journeying west toward she knew not what. And just then she did not want to think ahead. Having survived this terrifying day was enough.

From the next bench, Theo said, " 'They sailed upon a wine-dark sea.' "

"What?"

Theo gestured to the brownish water now turned to ink by the descending sun. "Readers of Homer have wondered for centuries what he meant by those words."

The second team leader surprised them all by saying in his deep voice, " 'And now I have put in here, as thou seest, with ship and crew, while sailing over the wine-dark sea to men of strange speech.' "

Theo revealed a truly lovely smile. "Well, what do you know."

"Hey, man." The second team leader's accent was stronger now. The word came out as *mon*. "Homer wrote his poetry with warriors in mind."

"You don't say."

"Absolute truth, what I'm telling you." He lifted the automatic rifle propped against his thigh. "If he were alive today, he'd have something beautiful to say about this."

Theo studied the man. "Can I ask your name?"

Two glanced to his left, where Bruno observed them from the inflatable craft. When their leader did not speak, he replied, "I am Henri."

"Nice to know you, Henri. I'm Theo. Thanks for saving our lives back there."

"All part of the service, man."

Theo gripped the bench to either side of where he sat and recited, " 'Sing, oh muse, of the rage of Achilles, son of Peleus, that brought countless ills upon the Aegeans.' "

Henri's smile grew broader still. He chanted the words, " 'Hateful to me as the gates of Hades is that man who hides one thing in his heart and speaks another.' "

Theo replied with, " 'Like the generations of leaves, the lives of mortal men. Now the wind scatters the old leaves across the earth, now the living timber bursts with the new buds and spring comes round again.' "

Henri almost sang the words, " 'Why so much grief for me? No man will hurl me down to Death, against my fate. And fate? No one alive has ever escaped it, neither brave man nor coward.' "

Theo responded, " 'Fool, prate not to me about covenants.' "

Henri joined in with him, and together they called to the first stars, " 'There can be no covenant between men and lions. Wolves and lambs can never be of one mind, but hate each other out and out and through. Therefore there can be no understanding between you and me, nor may there be any covenants between us, till one or other shall fall!' "

Their laughter spilled across the waters. Della thought they all traveled easier after this exchange. Even though they motored away from land, defying the death and danger that lurked just beyond the horizon.

Then a voice Della did not recognize came

through her earpiece. "Is this a private party or can anyone join in?"

Avery leaped to his feet, then had to be steadied by warriors' hands. "I know . . . that's Trevor!"

Della asked, "Who?"

"The skipper of the boat that brought me here!"

"Rule one of surviving combat," Bruno said. "Always keep a secret back door."

eleven

Theo had never been on a research vessel before. A female crew member led him down a steel causeway to a small single cabin. Everything was spotless, and the shower worked beautifully. The bathroom was so small he knocked up against the sink as he washed his hair. The drain was a simple hole in the middle of the whitewashed floor. Which explained why the towels had been set on the narrow bunk. He wiped the steamy mirror and inspected his face. Theo decided he looked exhausted. Which was hardly a surprise. Not after he had packed the weight of disappointment and defeat into days without beginning or end—only to be rescued at the very last moment by a brother he did not know at all.

They ate dinner in the crew's mess. A pair of portholes looked out over a black night. The ship's crew had already eaten. Theo, Avery, Della, and their security detail had the galley to themselves. The separation between Bruno's team and the three of them remained in place. Henri grinned at Theo as he departed. Otherwise there was no contact, nor anything spoken. Theo did not mind. Now that he was safe, the fatigue rested on him like a thousand-pound weight. Avery's hands trembled slightly as he lifted each mouthful. Della ate sparingly. She and Avery both spent the mealtime staring at scenes they painted on the opposite wall.

As they walked the corridor back to their cabins, Della surprised Theo with a touch on his arm. When he stopped, she waited as Avery and two of Bruno's crew continued down to their berths. The female soldier smirked at them before unlocking her door and stepping inside.

Once they were alone, Della said, "We need to talk."

"Can it wait? I really want to hear what you have to say. All of it. But I need to be awake for that. Right now I'm so tired it wouldn't register."

She gave a reluctant nod. "Rest well."

Theo slept as deeply as he had in his entire adult life. He woke with the disconcerted sensation of having no idea where he was or why his forehead rested against a painted steel wall. He showered again, trying to scrub away the odors of burning cordite and smoke rising from a silent town.

When he returned to the mess hall, the clock over the kitchen-access window read 10:14 a.m. Theo was glad Della was the only one seated there. She wore a sailor's T-shirt and denim shorts. Her feet were bare and her hair was still damp. Theo thought she looked stunning. She offered a tentative smile and said, "Coffee's in the urn, if you're interested."

"Desperate, more like." He filled a heavy

ceramic mug, added milk, and accepted the cook's offer of eggs and toast. "May I join you?"

She waited until he seated himself, then said, "Avery's spoken by sat phone with his wife and kids. He was pretty broken up afterward. He's back in his room, resting." She pointed to a plastic case on the table. "Bruno left it there in case you want to reach out and touch base with someone."

"Thanks. But there isn't anyone except my brother. And I want to give myself a little while longer to work through what just happened."

Della rocked her mug in a little circle and waited as the cook's mate brought over a plate and silverware. As Theo started eating, she said, "There's something I need to tell you. Only I don't know how."

"Take your time and start from the beginning," he replied. "It's always worked best for me."

"I'd basically be putting my professional life in your hands, doing that."

He set down his fork. Wiped his mouth. Took his time, waiting until she lifted her worried gaze. "Della, there's no way I can say it clearer than this. I'm not my brother. Whatever you tell me stays between us."

She took a long breath. Nodded once. "Everything you think you know about why I'm here, working with Bishop Industries, is a lie."

• • •

There was a surreal quality to the conversation that followed. Or rather, to sitting there and listening while Della talked. On one level, the longer Theo was in this woman's company, the more he felt drawn to her. On another, what she told him would define a scandal in the making, if he actually represented his brother's company. Which he didn't. But more important still, he felt them moving into sync. It was an illogical sensation, given what she was saying. Even so, he listened to Della reveal her secrets and felt his own brother gradually coming into focus.

Della spoke in a voice deepened by shame. The confession cost her terribly. Theo found himself as impacted by her willingness to come clean as by what she told him.

She had studied business with a minor in journalism. She had always had a head for figures and intended to go into accounting in graduate school, acquire her CPA license, and make a comfortable if somewhat boring existence for herself. But she had also enjoyed writing, and while in school she had submitted a couple of pieces to the Baltimore paper. These had led to a job offer, and soon Della found herself enthralled by the world of journalism. Yet her employer faced the same financial troubles as most other newspapers of late, and being a recent hire, Della was the first to go.

The problem was, by that point she knew she wanted to continue as a reporter. The only journalistic work she could find was writing for an online business blog. The pay was awful, and the work was often demeaning. Della tried to convince herself it was a temporary gig. Three years later, she was still sending out résumés and hunting down journalistic crumbs.

Then she had been struck by the big idea. The one that might just fast-track her into a real journalistic position. She had applied for a job in Bishop Industries' PR department. And she was hired. She worked as hard as she ever had in her entire life and was promoted as a result. Four times. Until she was finally in a position to start doing her *real* work—hunting for the company's ties to illegal activities. The ones often rumored about but never proven. Bishop Industries was squeaky clean these days, but in years past rumors had swirled about Kenneth Bishop secretly owning shares of opioid outlets through bogus holding companies. And paying bribes to doctors. And overcharging Medicare through unscrupulous clinics and hospitals. And so forth. She was now senior enough to begin scouring old records. It was time to make her move.

Della had approached the business editor at the *Washington Post* and been offered a freelance contract with the understanding that if she delivered the goods, the position would become permanent.

But then the editor went on maternity leave, and her replacement was a numbers cruncher who disliked Della and the whole concept of taking her on. Since their very first meeting, Jerry had been looking for a reason to revoke her contract and cast her adrift.

Della reached this point in her telling and just stopped. Her head had gradually lowered as she talked, until her hair formed a dark veil that completely blocked her face from view.

Theo wished there were some reason to keep things as they were right now. The two of them deep inside a steel-hulled vessel plying the Atlantic off the western coast of Africa. Della talking, and him leaning against the inner wall. Just loving the look and sound of this woman.

He knew there was no way he could simply say the words, that what she told him didn't really matter all that much. That her subterfuge was unimportant as far as he was concerned. She probably wouldn't believe him. Theo was, after all, brother to the reason why she was involved at all.

So he said, "Truth for truth. All right?"

Della did not look up. Which was a shame. He could dive into those blue-gray eyes and swim forever. She nodded at the table between her hands.

A couple of the ship's crew came in, talking loudly. Theo shifted around so that he sat closer to her, near enough to lean in and make sure what he said was for her ears alone. He began, "What impacts me the most is that you need to tell me at all. And that touches a very deep level."

While she did not look up at him, Theo could tell she was paying careful attention. He went on, "I made this journey partly because I wanted to repay Kenny for bailing out my company. It was the only thing he asked in return. The first thing he had *ever* asked of me. Plus, I thought it would be a real kick. An adventure. And after the year I've had, it appealed to me more than I could possibly say."

Della leaned back and studied him. "But that isn't the real reason, is it?"

He liked the sense that they were in sync now. That somehow she had already figured out where he was going. "I don't know my brother. At all. Before, I had a reason not to care. Now . . ."

Avery and one of Bruno's team came in then and started toward their table. Della turned to them and said, "Could you sit somewhere else, please?" After they moved off, she said to Theo, "Go on."

"We are seeing fragments of a puzzle," Theo replied. "And part of why we can't put it all together is, we're looking at the wrong Kenny."

Della opened her mouth, stopped, closed it

again. Holding back on whatever it was she was about to say.

"The Kenny I knew as a kid, the Kenneth Bishop you were hired by the *Post* to investigate, is not the same guy who sent us here. To Africa."

She nodded slowly. "That almost makes sense."

"The only way we can understand what's happening here is if we start over," Theo said.

"Do you really believe people can change that much?"

"Until all this began, I would have said no. Definitely not."

"Small shifts, sure," Della said. "But such a seismic revolt as this? A businessman known for his ruthless killer instincts becomes . . . What has he become?"

It was Theo's turn to nod. Rocking his entire body. Feeling that closely in sync with her. "That is the question we have to answer. It's the only way we'll ever figure out what's going on."

twelve

They left the galley together as the ship's crew started arriving for their midday meal. Theo asked Della to bring Avery upstairs to the main deck. He wanted to speak with Bruno. Then the three of them needed to talk.

The bow area was larger than Theo's house and lined with fiberglass lockers bolted to the steel deck. The starboard side was dominated by a massive crane-and-winch system, with two boats stored on either side. The dinghy and inflatable that had carried them here were both lashed to the stern. Clearly this was a highly functional vessel, operated by a man who paid attention to safety and detail. Bruno, Henri, and two crew members had spread out a tarp beneath the pilot's cabin and were field-stripping weapons. Theo asked, "Where are we headed?"

"Port of Bissau is our first choice." Bruno wiped a rag down the length of a rifle barrel, then peered into the muzzle. "But the situation is fluid. We'll know more before we arrive. All flights from the Bissau airport to Europe were canceled last month. The troops on airport duty took a bribe from a human trafficker and forced the paying passengers off an Air Portugal flight sitting on the runway. They loaded in a group of

Syrian refugees and ordered the pilots at gunpoint to fly them all to Lisbon."

Theo squatted down next to the tarp. "I actually don't know what to say to that."

"Trevor claims the situation in the capital is back under control." Bruno pointed to the mirrored glass shielding the cockpit from view. "Supposedly the European flights are operating again. But we won't know for certain until we get there."

"Please tell me you won't be dumping us and flying off to your next gig."

Henri grinned as he ratcheted the trigger mechanism back into place. "Don't fret yourself, man. Worry is a big part of our job."

Della appeared from the interior shadows, leading Avery. Theo stood and asked, "How long until we arrive?"

Bruno pointed toward a green shadow on the eastern horizon. "Three hours before we're port-side. We'll need another hour to check things out. Then you can disembark."

Theo stepped away from the crew and motioned for Della and Avery to join him by the bow rail. He could see by the tentative way the scientist approached that Avery remained trapped in the fear of what they had just left behind. And what it all might mean for his future.

Theo told him, "It's really important that you hear what I'm about to say. I am on your side. No matter what. After all we've been through, I hope you'll accept this as the truth."

Avery tasted the air. His overlarge larynx bobbed up and down a couple of times. His chin trembled slightly.

Theo said, "You're a scientist. I don't need to talk to you about how to fashion your study."

"There's nothing to work on," Avery said. "I lost all my samples. The data we were collecting, the computers we stored our findings on. Gone."

Theo suppressed a smile. The guy had just survived a firefight. In Africa. And what upset Avery most was losing his test results. "We have a new issue. A mystery that's tied to where we've just come from. And I'm hoping you'll help us solve it. For this to work, we need to be clear about something. Two things, actually. I am absolutely certain that my brother was a cutthroat assassin when it came to his business practices. He took no prisoners. It was all about the bottom line. Do I think he was previously involved in promoting the opioid epidemic? Yes, I do. I've no evidence to support it, but I think that it's probably all true."

They were both watching him intently now.

"Point two. Something has changed. Something in my brother is different. Otherwise none of this makes any sense. The cost of this operation, setting you up with a lab. In Africa. Bringing us here. This ship. Bruno's crew. None of this is the work of a man whose only concern is increasing profits. Either he's changed or . . ."

"The deaths," Della said. "It's not just about those villages."

Avery turned to her. "Why are you here?"

"I wish I knew. I'm in the company's marketing department."

Avery stared at her. "I don't understand. Mr. Bishop sent somebody from PR to a crisis zone?"

"The question is, why did he send *anybody.*" Theo looked from one to the other. "Kenny suspected we would be facing something really, really big. He has an idea, a shred of evidence, a rumor, news of some report. Something. And it terrifies him. So he's sent you, Avery, to find the key linking everything together."

"But I failed."

"Hold that thought. And you, Della, you're here because he wants to have someone who can now get the word out to a global audience."

"A warning."

"If he's right. If it's real," Theo agreed.

"And what about you?"

"He's sending his wife and children to Asheville. He's bailed out my failing company. He's asked me to get my team ready. Just in case."

Della asked, "In case of *what?*"

"Exactly. That's what we have to discover. So here's what I want you to consider. That we stop letting Kenny pull our strings. We decide who, when, and what. We work together. As a team."

Della thought Theo's delivery was stellar. A genuine man laying out what he thought was the best way for them to move forward. She admired him for being so honest. It was hard, she knew from experience, to express something with such conviction when there was every chance the reality was very different. She had been in this position too often. Trying to convince editors that they should invest in a concept that could very well prove to be totally wrong. Theo spoke with a raw honesty that touched her deeply. She could see he wanted Avery to stay with them through whatever came next. But Theo also wanted the scientist's involvement to be founded upon truth.

But Della could also see that Avery was not convinced. The scientist remained trapped inside a fear and tension and fatigue so potent, Della was not sure how much Avery actually heard. His entire body remained clenched. His grip on the railing turned his knuckles bloodless.

If Theo noticed Avery's nerves, he did not show it. His voice remained casual as he asked, "How often have you spoken with Kenny?"

"Three times." Avery wrestled with the railing. "The first time, he called me in the middle of the night. A recent report I submitted confirmed something he'd heard from another source. He didn't want to tell me anything more, because he wanted me to examine the evidence unclouded by what were still just rumors. Then he sent me out here."

Theo was rocking now, back and forth. But instead of tension, Della could see the news genuinely excited him. "After that?"

"I phoned him when we returned to this boat after discovering the fishermen. Mr. Bishop asked what we had done with the bodies. Like it was the most natural thing in the world to find nineteen fishing vessels with no one alive in them. I told him the skipper had fired the boats. He said he wanted me to go onshore and identify the illness that had caused this. I said no, I wasn't . . ." Avery sighed, reliving the argument in his head.

"What did my brother tell you?"

"He offered to give me whatever new position I wanted. And a half-million-dollar bonus. If I could identify the infectious strain. But I couldn't. And now I want to go home."

"I know you do." Theo took hold of the railing too. "When was the third time?"

"Just now. But I didn't speak with him. I phoned his private cell number like he instructed, and this lawyer answered."

"Preston Borders," Theo said.

"Right. He asked me to stay and assist you in your efforts." Avery glowered at him. "But you're not a scientist, are you?"

"I'm a professor of economics."

"So you don't have a clue." Avery released a tight tremor. "I've never seen anything like . . . I'm scared."

"You probably should be," Theo agreed. "The danger is very real. And if I'm right, the threats won't end just because we're out of Senegal."

"Why are you telling me this?" Avery's voice rose to a near yell. "I'm a *scientist*. I work inside a *lab*."

"Because you need to make a choice based on the reality of our situation," Theo replied. "While you still can. Before the next threat takes hold."

"No." Avery chopped the air between them. "I'm *out*." He scurried across the bow, wrenched open the metal door, then shouted at them, "I'm *finished* with this. You can send me samples. Or not. Right now I don't care. I just want to go *home*."

Theo stared at the open doorway, clearly disappointed. "This isn't good. We need him."

"We'll find another scientist, if we have to," Della replied.

He looked at her. "*We'll* find a scientist."

"That's right. I'm in. For what it's worth, I thought you were right on target. So what comes next?"

"We need to speak with the captain."

She followed him up the exterior stairs and through the door and into the cockpit's cool wash.

Trevor stood by the front windows, scouting the green shoreline. The skipper lowered his binoculars and said in greeting, "I've ordered a fresh set of clothes laid out in your cabins. And a razor for you, Dr. Bishop."

"Mind if I ask a couple of questions?"

Trevor went back to searching the way ahead. "Long as you make it snappy. The Bissau port's only tug has broken down."

The woman standing on duty by the wheel said, "The harbormaster's drunk, most likely."

"Whatever. We have to berth on our own. The shoals along this coastline shift constantly."

Theo asked, "When my brother booked your vessel, what exactly were your orders?"

"Correction. I was not hired by Bishop Industries. I have never even spoken to anyone from that group."

"So who hired you?"

"I was specifically ordered by my owners not to ask."

"Any idea why?"

"I don't like to speculate when it might risk my paycheck."

Up ahead, Della watched islands gradually separating themselves from the mainland, and then a wide green delta came into view. She heard Theo ask, "So then what were your orders?"

"Simple enough. Take Dr. Avery Madison to the Casamance delta. Do whatever he told us to do and then bring him back. After we found the fishing vessels, we received new orders to drop him off. Then a third set of orders arrived, telling us to hold off the coast."

"But Avery didn't know you were still on duty when Bruno brought us out."

Trevor nodded. "Control of this vessel was shifted to Bruno. He told us to lay well off the Casamance River mouth, tell no one, and maintain radio silence."

"Who transferred control to Bruno?"

"An interesting question," Trevor said, "and the answer is, I have no idea. I received a cable from our headquarters in Fort Lauderdale. It's part of the ship's log now, if you want to check it out."

"No, that's okay. Thanks." Theo squinted at the approaching line of green.

"Was that all?"

"Just one more question. Are there ocean currents that bind together the different continents?"

All of the crew were watching him now. Trevor said, "That's another interesting question."

"I'll take that as a yes."

"Absolutely. In the days of sailing vessels, ocean crossings were set to the calendar of wind and currents. In these waters, the seasonal trade winds are matched by three currents, strong as rivers. These are the northern and southern equatorials, and the Benguela Current." He pointed to his right. "Farther south runs a fourth, the mother of all currents, the Circumpolar Arctic. That one goes right around the world. Its proper name is the Thermohaline Circulation. People in our line of work call it the 'great conveyor belt.' A billion gallons a month, according to the latest reckoning."

"Do all seagoing captains know this?"

"Highly unlikely. But this is a research vessel. I'm obliged to know more than most." Trevor lifted the binoculars. "Now you'll need to excuse me. I'm about to get very busy keeping my ship afloat."

Theo thanked him and ushered Della outside. When the door closed behind them, he asked, "Did you get the impression he wanted to avoid telling us something?"

"I don't . . . maybe."

Theo stayed where he was, two steps down. "Will you do something for me? Use the sat phone and call Kenny's office. Ask to speak with my brother, tell whoever answers that it's urgent."

"What should I tell Kenneth?"

Theo hesitated long enough for the individual palms lining the shore to become visible. Finally he said, "If they connect you with Kenny, lay out the facts. Ask him what we should do next. But my gut tells me you won't be given that chance."

thirteen

Della placed the call, then returned to her cabin to shower and change clothes. She emerged wearing another ship's uniform of a white T-shirt with the vessel's name and logo on the pocket, white canvas deck shoes, and pale jeans. No belt and no jewelry except the watch she'd worn on the trip over. Her passport was in her back pocket. The clothes she'd been wearing had been washed but were left unironed, stowed now in a ship's canvas carryall. Everything else she'd brought with her from America was in a plane somewhere. She made a mental note to ask Bruno about that, but for the moment, simply being here alive and safe was enough to make the location of her suitcase and makeup and laptop and other personal effects just so extremely unimportant.

She found Theo seated on a bench on the main deck. The cockpit's overhang offered shade, but the heat was still fierce. He wore an outfit identical to her own. She seated herself next to him and said, "I assume we're dressed okay for the flight home."

He gave her a long look. "You turn those clothes into a fashion statement."

She liked having a reason to smile. "Well thanks, sailor."

"Did you speak with Kenny?"

"No, as a matter of fact. I was patched into some lawyer's office."

"Preston Borders." Theo bounded to his feet. "What did he say?"

"He listened to my report. He asked what we intended to do next. I told him we were coming home. Borders wants you to call him. Then he hung up." She watched him rock back and forth on his feet, heel to toe, almost dancing in place. "Is that good?"

"It confirms something. I think." He held up his hand. "Don't ask me anything yet. Please. I need . . ."

Theo stopped because Avery walked over. His expression was funereal. "Claudia says I have to help."

Theo continued rocking. "And Claudia is . . . ?"

"My wife." Avery's oversized larynx bobbed once. "I called her to say I was done with this. That I was coming home and we could restart our lives."

Theo grinned. "What did your wife tell you?"

"She wouldn't even let me finish. She ordered me to come back and tell you that I was in. For our kids' future." Avery shook his head. "She doesn't get angry very often. When she does . . ."

"Remind me to thank her," Theo said. "First chance I get."

• • •

"Hello?"

"Susan, it's Della."

"Oh, hey, I'm sorry I didn't get back to you." The *Post*'s former business editor coughed. "But the baby's had the flu, and then she gave it to both me and Harry."

"I need to talk with you about Jerry."

"I know he's a pain, but there's really not much I can do." Susan's fatigue inserted a grainy roughness to her normally sultry, smooth voice. Like she had become so weary she had forgotten what it was like to be fresh or alert or rested. "It's Jerry's department now. They've already warned that when I come back, I'll be reassigned to another—"

Della cut in with, "I'm going to call him when you and I stop talking. Jerry will probably fire me. I want you to know my side. That's all."

She filled in her former boss as quickly as she could. Less than two minutes, start to finish.

Susan Glass was a heavyset woman with a debutante's manner, very prim and polite, her Greenville upbringing lacing every word with a honeyed Southern accent. Even now, when she was brutally tired. "Where are you calling me from now?"

"On the boat that rescued us from Casamance. Entering the river mouth leading to the Port of Bissau."

"Spell those places for me, would you, dear?" In the distance, a baby began crying. Susan lowered the phone and called, "See to her, please. I'm on the phone. Thank you, darling." She came back on with, "What are you going to do now?"

"Soon as I'm done with Jerry, Theo is going to contact his brother. We're starting over."

"Well, I don't see how you have any choice. Not with all the lab samples back there in the burning village."

"I'm not talking about just the disease or whatever it is. I mean we're restarting the investigation of Kenneth Bishop. Something's happening, Susan. This is much bigger than a question of whether Kenneth once owned part shares in opioid pill mills. We need to get to the bottom of why he's become so concerned with a problem on the other side of the world."

Susan went quiet. The sat phone hissed softly as if sharing their tension. Della felt a warm breeze filter through her hair, drying the sweat almost as swiftly as it formed. They were surrounded now by numerous other vessels. Most of the freighters held the wretched look of rust and age and countless hard voyages. The river mouth was several miles wide here, the stretch of water dotted with islands. Many held oil-exploration rigs, their triangular shapes rising like misbegotten metal trees. Della watched as a wooden canoe pushed in front of their ship. The four paddlers strained against the current, while between them rose a pile of cassava roots high as a man.

Finally, Susan asked, "You haven't spoken with Jerry?"

"Not yet."

"Let me have a word with the fourth floor." The fourth was home to the senior administrative staff. As in, Jerry's boss.

"Thank you so much."

"I can't promise you anything, dear. Jerry is not so much the problem as a symbol of what's facing us all."

"I understand."

"Call me in an hour. No, better yet, call me when you have something new to report. Don't speak with Jerry until you and I have talked. And Della?"

"Yes?"

"Do try and come back alive, will you, dear?"

As Theo listened to Della's conversation with her former boss, he wished there were some way he could hit a giant pause button and let them step off the course they were on. Not for long, just a few days, a week at most. Enough for them to get to know each other, to see if what he felt was real. If they might have a chance. Together.

Della ended the conversation and offered him the phone. "She told me not to call Jerry."

Theo struggled to focus on the now. "What is Jerry's exact title?"

"Acting editor of the business section. I'm told he is very good with numbers."

Theo took the phone but stayed as he was, studying her. "I think you should switch over and become an employee of my company. We could name you head of our new marketing and PR section. If anyone asks, it's part of the agreement we made for Kenny to bail us out. Your new job description will include researching this whole deal and then reporting on it. We'll put it in your contract."

The look she gave him was intense, like she was trying to figure out exactly who he was. "Can I think on that?"

"Take as long as you like. In the meantime, can you connect me to Kenny's office?"

"You don't have his number?"

"I told you, Della. Before all this started, I hadn't spoken with Kenny in over four years."

Della punched in the number, listened, then handed the phone back in time for Theo to hear a woman say, "Mr. Bishop's office."

"This is Theo Bishop. I need—"

"Yes, Dr. Bishop. Hold just a moment, please."

Theo stood watching the swarm of smaller vessels plying the greenish-brown waters. The Bissau River delta was far broader than the Casamance, the traffic very heavy. He liked the smells that drifted in the humid air, pushing gently beneath the canvas awning that shielded them from the sun. Diesel fumes from the boats, fish, cooking fires, even the sweet funk emanating from the refuse dotting the shoreline—the combination of it all was utterly alien, intense, and very exciting to him.

The phone emitted a louder *click,* and then a man's voice said, "Dr. Bishop?"

"Yes."

"Preston Borders here. Where are you?"

"Coming into the Port of Bissau. Why are we speaking?"

"Your brother is dealing with an unexpected crisis. He wanted me to ask if you might be willing to meet with an associate of his in Bissau."

"It's why we came here, isn't it? Instead of heading somewhere safer. Kenny wanted me to have this meeting."

"Quite so. That is, if you are indeed interested in proceeding further."

Theo listened to the sat phone's faint electric hiss and felt the tension pass through the device, along his arm, and begin to fill his body. "I am. Absolutely. Interested."

"Splendid. Your brother will be delighted with this news. Do you have a pen and paper?"

Avery complained, "I don't see what possible good this can do. I've lost all my samples. Every possible means of determining—"

“Forget your samples,” Theo told him.

“I . . . What?”

They were motoring away from the research vessel, which was anchored about fifty meters off the harbor wall. The river here was broad as an inland sea. The opposite bank was a distant smudge. Up ahead, soldiers lounged beneath tarps that protected piles of fresh produce. The eyes that watched their approach were not friendly. Theo thought Avery had every possible reason to be nervous.

Theo said, “If your samples had the information you required, we’d already have the answer. Right?”

Avery stared at him. Confused. As if he couldn’t place who was speaking.

“The samples don’t have our answer. By the time you showed up, the danger was gone.”

“You can’t possibly know that with any certainty.” Avery’s objection sounded feeble.

It was Della who said, “The soldiers.”

“Right. None of them wore protective gear,” Theo said.

“They had just arrived,” Avery protested.

Theo was being handed every possible reason to dislike the scientist. The guy was a walking bundle of geeky nerves. Taking him from the lab was like watching a goldfish flop outside its aquarium. But none of it mattered. Theo had been around people like Avery all his academic life.

They were trained to examine one tiny aspect of the real world, and through one specific lens. Avery was a microbiologist, which meant he was probably the best there was at anything smaller than an individual germ. Put him in the field, with its grime and danger, and he freaked. He had no coping mechanism for the uncontrollable elements of life. Of course he was afraid.

Theo said, "The fishing boats tell us what we need to know about timing. You described how they were filled with locals who had set off for just another day on the waters. They were felled with something that struck so fast they couldn't get back to shore. Whatever it is that's making people sick, by the time we arrived it was long gone. That means your samples didn't hold the answer."

They traveled with Henri and the lone member of the security team who knew Bissau. According to Bruno, Simone had been born in the capital and left when she was nine. She was a small woman with limbs of dark iron. She crouched in the dinghy's bow, watching the approaching harbor wall with unblinking intensity. The two security guards were armed with pepper spray and side arms. A third man was seated by Henri, there to wait and guard the boat. An automatic rifle was propped by his right knee.

Avery said quietly, "I knew that."

"Of course you did."

Della asked Simone, “Do you speak the local lingo?”

“Portuguese, yes.” Simone’s gaze did not shift away from the approaching dock. “And my father’s tongue, Balanta.”

The odors were fierce. The soldiers lining the dock watched them with stony faces. Henri motored up to a set of slimy stairs cut into the harbor wall. The security held the boat in place while they disembarked. Simone climbed the stairs with Henri next. Theo waited with Della and Avery on the broad stone platform as the third security motored the dinghy back into the channel.

One of the local troops said something, half question and half demand. As Simone responded, Henri showed a pale palm holding a stack of US dollars. The soldiers and Simone went back and forth several times before one of them turned and walked away. Another shook Henri’s hand and made the dollars disappear.

Henri said to Theo, “You can come up now.”

They stood like that, Simone conversing with the soldiers in a soft liquid tongue, while the sun beat down. Theo could feel the stench working its way into his pores. Finally, Avery asked, “Is there any reason we’re not standing over there in the shade?”

Henri did not look over as he replied, “Yes.”

A few minutes later, a military truck pulled up.

At a gesture from Henri, they piled into the back with Simone. Henri squeezed himself into the front seat. With a word from the soldier who had accepted the money, they set off.

Once they were under way, Simone said, “This is the safest way for us to travel. We pay one bribe before, one when we return. The troops we bribe accompany us through the city. Safely.”

Bissau was a combination of derelict colonial buildings and newer structures in drastic need of repair. The streets they took were broad and straight and mostly dirt. The asphalt and cobblestones of some earlier epoch formed ragged lumps that their truck mostly avoided. They shared the roads with donkey carts and ancient blue taxis and thousands of mopeds. The noise was as fierce as the smells.

They entered a chaotic central market, turned down a side street, and halted before a whitewashed wall. The entry was topped by a curved lintel where words had once been inscribed. A young man slouched in the entryway while a boy sat just outside, using an upturned plastic pail as a chair. As soon as the military truck halted, a pair of beggars loitering just beyond the boy scurried away. Simone stepped down, spoke a few words to the young man, and pointed at Theo. At a word from the man, the boy rose and disappeared through the portal. Simone gestured for them to climb down.

The courtyard beyond the entryway was mostly swept dirt with little graveled pathways lined by whitewashed stones. More painted stones encircled trees and neat flower beds. A trio of young girls in brightly colored shifts were pouring water from buckets over the blossoms. Theo could see five buildings and assumed there were more, all of them tidy-looking, single-storied with tiled roofs, and white. The compound was perhaps three acres in size. Beyond the farthest buildings, Theo spotted workers tending a vegetable garden. He heard the crow of a rooster. The young man pointed them to a bench beneath a jacaranda tree and went back to guarding the front gate.

The compound was an island of calm within the city's din. Through open windows, Theo saw figures in white uniforms walk around beds arranged in orderly rows. He had never been comfortable around sick people. The idea of sacrificing the years required to become a doctor so that he could spend his life in a hospital was baffling to him.

Theo sat in the wall's shade and recalled how, when his mother had become ill that last time, he had forced himself to be there for her. His father was already gone, felled by a stroke. Theo's brother had visited the hospital once and then come a second time to the hospice center, but Kenny had spent most of both visits on his phone. After the funeral, Theo had watched as Kenny rushed to the limo idling by the curb, already back on his phone. It was the last time he had seen his brother until the chopper had landed at Fairview.

And now this.

Avery broke into his thoughts by muttering, "I still don't get why we're here."

Theo could not tell whether he meant the clinic or the city. Or maybe just Africa in general. "Just be ready."

"For what?"

As if in reply, a middle-aged African woman with a stethoscope draped around her neck stepped through the central building's doorway. A man in hospital whites followed, pressing her to look at the clipboard he carried. She glanced down, scribbled her name, barked at him, then turned to where the boy stood pointing in their direction. Theo rose to his feet as she started toward them. Everything about her shouted impatience and drive and intelligence. She demanded, "Yes, what do you want?"

"Dr. Lanica Amadou?"

"I'm very busy today. If you're donors, I'm grateful for your interest. One of my assistants will show you around. You can also find everything you need to know on our website—"

"My name is Theo Bishop. Kenny is my brother."

She squinted at him, almost angry in her intensity. “Yes, I see the resemblance. But I still fail to understand—”

“We’ve just come from the Casamance.”

There was a genuine shift this time. The stressed and focused woman stopped dead in her tracks. “And?”

“Both of the port towns are gone. Everyone is dead. Humans, animals, the lot.”

“Do you have any idea of the cause?”

Avery answered this time. “Colds. Measles. Septicemia. Nothing that can explain the level of fatalities.”

“In that case, we need to talk.” She glanced at her watch. “I have two crucial surgeries that can’t wait. Go have a meal. I’ll join you when I can.”

fourteen

Della followed Theo and Avery into the communal hall. The young man who had greeted them at the front portal now stood in the broad window leading into the kitchen. When he spotted them, he turned and spoke to someone Della could not see. An older woman whose graying curls were tied with myriad blue strings smiled and waved at them. She and the young man disappeared. A few minutes later, they reappeared through a swinging door, both bearing trays.

The woman demanded, "Which of you is brother to Mr. Kenneth?"

"That would be me."

She set down her tray and enfolded Theo in her two massive arms. "Your brother, sir, he is a saint."

Della could see the news rocked Theo in a way that the flying bullets had not. When he remained silent, Della asked, "Mr. Kenneth helps with this clinic?"

"Everything you see here, it is his work. You have visited Mr. Kenneth's operating theater?"

The young man spoke English for the first time. "Dr. Lanica has surgeries."

"Of course she does. Dr. Lanica, she is another saint."

Della thought she saw a mischievous glint in the woman's eye. "But a very pushy one, no?"

The woman released a musical laugh. "You know her well already."

"So you're saying Dr. Lanica is one woman you do not want to see angry?"

The young man joined in the laughter. He said, "We have a special burn unit just for those poor people."

Theo seemed confused by the conversation, like he was trying to piece together words from an unknown tongue. Della asked, "Dr. Lanica is American?"

"Oh my, no. She is born right here in the Bissau market town."

The young man said, "Dr. Lanica, she studied surgery in America."

"Our good doctor has many gifts," the woman added. "Healing, language, many gifts."

"But not patience."

They both laughed. Then the young man said, "We all must wait until heaven offers us the missing pieces, no?"

The woman said, "Dr. Lanica, she speaks seven languages."

"Six," the young man corrected. "Creole is not a language, Dr. Lanica says. It is a stew."

"I give you stew." The woman passed out crude clay bowls. "This is *egusi.* You taste."

Della took a tentative spoonful. It was spicy,

and oddly flavored, but incredible. “This is wonderful.”

The woman beamed. “Groundnuts, tree seeds, black-eyed peas. Mr. Kenneth, he loves my egusi. He can sit there and eat four bowls.”

The young man set out a plate of what appeared to be uncooked bread dough. “This is *fufu*. You will like.”

“Cassava and green plantain flour,” the woman said. “Make a small ball, dip into the stew.”

Della did as they instructed and declared, “Delicious.”

The young man straightened and lost his smile. “Dr. Lanica is here.”

The old woman hugged Theo a second time. “You tell Mr. Kenneth that Hetta the cook prays for him and Sister Amelia. Every night she prays.”

Della liked how this visit had helped clarify her new direction. She had spent almost a year researching Kenneth Bishop and his involvement in the opioid crisis. The evidence that had drawn Della into this investigation still remained true. She had not been fooled. She knew Bishop’s corporate past in and out.

His *past*.

But here she sat, surrounded by a present that did not fit with the pattern or the man she thought she knew. Which meant she had to accept that the impossible had happened. They were surrounded by evidence that Kenneth Bishop had undergone a drastic shift. She could not sit here, in this clinic, and think otherwise.

Hetta brought another bowl of stew and saucer of fufu. She set down both in front of the doctor and patted Theo's shoulder as she departed. After Lanica bowed her head over the food, she started eating with the same sharp gestures as apparently she did everything. Finally, she said, "There are three more surgeries slated for this afternoon. A public clinic this evening. I only have a few minutes."

Avery asked, "What do you call this disease?"

"It's too early to use that word. Disease suggests a specific cause-and-effect set of circumstances. They might exist. They might not."

Della liked the doctor's method of speaking. Lanica's responses might have sounded impatient as bullets, but they were also very clear. She would, Della suspected, have made an excellent teacher. "We need a name."

Lanica fashioned a small ball of fufu and scooped out some of the stew before responding. "Some of my colleagues are calling it *Lupa.* That's the Portuguese word for bloom." Another bite, then, "In our not-so-distant past, it was also the local slang for leprosy, another disease no one understood for far too long."

Della reached into her pocket for the pad and pen she'd taken from the ship. "Do you mind if I take notes?"

fifteen

Theo felt assaulted by all the evidence of a brother he did not know. Glancing around the lovely commons hall, with the red tiled floor, the big windows framed in stained glass, and the exposed beams and the crosses over every doorway . . . all of this represented something else entirely.

What Theo mostly saw were years of lost opportunities.

He thought back to the times Kenny had phoned him over the past few years. Theo had simply assumed Kenny wanted to brag about his newest acquisition. He had marked Kenny's incoming emails as spam for the same reason. But now he sat surrounded by evidence that, during those missing years, Kenny had become someone else.

This new Kenneth had traveled to Africa. He had become a beloved figure by these people. He was an ally to a group whose sole purpose was to help and heal and save lives. What Theo saw as he looked around was that Kenny had become a brother worthy of knowing. Of loving. A brother Theo had never even dared to wish he might have.

He heard the doctor say, "Following the Ghanaian outbreak, you know what I'm talking about, yes?"

"Of course," Avery replied. "The Ebola epidemic."

"The last time colleagues of mine gathered for a regional meeting, we set up an unofficial chat room. Adding anyone new could only be done after two or more of our unit met them in person. All communication regarding discoveries was limited to this one channel."

Avery jerked back from the table. "Wait, you're saying you had *advance warning?*"

"Let's stay on target here." She continued to talk between bites. "Our chat room is open only to clinicians we know and trust. It doesn't have a name. There's no link allowed to anything outside. It's not the dark web, but we share a lot of the same traits. Security is tight."

Della asked, "You're saying governments or international agencies are opposed to your talking?"

Lanica grimaced as she rolled another ball of fufu. "That's a western type of question. Everybody in my line of work remains directly tied to groups beyond our national borders. Funding, supplies, they all go through various channels. These are vital to our existence. We deal with them on a daily basis."

Della nodded. "You can't risk upsetting them."

Avery protested, "I don't see why you can't answer my question."

"She's trying to." Della did not take her eyes

off the doctor. "But first we have to understand her position."

Dr. Lanica Amadou smiled. Her entire visage went from sparking with anger to easygoing. "What was your name again?"

"Della Haverty."

"And you are connected to this how exactly?"

"Officially I'm in the PR department." Della took a hard breath. "But I also work as a journalist."

Theo found himself regretting how swiftly the smile vanished. Lanica snapped, "This must stay totally *off the record*."

"I understand. It will. You have my word."

The doctor continued to squint across the table. "Why should I trust you?"

"Kenneth Bishop does. Otherwise I wouldn't be here."

Theo cleared his throat and spoke for the first time since sitting down. "I trust her as well. Totally."

The doctor nodded once, tilted her bowl, and spooned out the last bites. She asked, "Where was I?"

"Funding and supplies," Della prompted.

"You listen. Good." Lanica pushed her bowl to one side. "Which means our work is very politically charged."

Avery complained, "That makes no sense. Why would a government or health organization object to your stopping an outbreak before it becomes a crisis?"

Lanica's smile returned, tighter this time. But Theo liked the gleam in her dark gaze and how she remained focused on Della. The journalist.

Della said, "It's not about the crisis. It's about what comes before and after. The impact *beyond* the health issue."

Lanica's smile reached her eyes. "You must be a very good journalist."

"I think so," Della replied.

Lanica turned to the scientist. "The OECD estimates that the Ebola virus outbreak cost the Ghanaian economy six and a half billion dollars in lost revenue, mostly tourism and industrial investment that went elsewhere. That's almost fifteen percent of the country's entire annual income. African nations are terrified of being seen as the center of a new epidemic."

Della nodded slowly. "Being *seen*."

"Exactly."

"So this is about *appearances*."

Avery said, "This is nuts, is what it is. We're talking about saving lives."

Della and Lanica just sat there, watching each other.

Avery shook his head. "I'm the only one who saw those people. I know what this thing can do. It's a killer of the first order and—"

"People die all the time," Della said. "What's the life expectancy in Guinea-Bissau?"

"Just over fifty," Lanica answered. "We're working on improving that."

"But to do this work you need outside help."

"Outside *funding,*" Lanica corrected. "Outside *supplies*."

"Right. And if there's an outbreak?"

"The western organizations come in and take over."

"All the funding goes toward halting this crisis."

Avery protested, "But this *is* a crisis!"

"Who says?" Lanica asked.

"*I* do. *We* do."

"One lone western scientist. Talking about people dying from . . . what was it you found?"

Della replied, "The flu."

Lanica asked Avery, "Do you think these national governments will just sit on their hands while you cry to the world about people dying from bad colds?"

"But the WHO—"

"You think the World Health Organization exists out there, totally disconnected from all these nations? Why do you think there is such fierce infighting for the top posts?"

"For funding," Della said. "For control of information."

"For everything," Lanica confirmed, still

watching Avery. "And you want to endanger this by putting out an alert. For which there is no hard evidence, other than a couple of villages that have been struck by bad colds."

"And the measles," Della added.

"They will do everything in their power to keep *potential* outbreaks from becoming the next bad headline," Lanica said.

"Which is why you set up your chat room," Della said. "An unofficial channel to discuss health issues at their very earliest stages."

"We cover numerous elements in these online conversations." Lanica turned her attention back to Della. "We discuss drugs we have on hand or that can be easily obtained, and how they might be used for treatment of diseases not listed in the official protocols."

"Which is totally prohibited," Della said.

"In the West," Lanica corrected. "Not allowed in *western* nations."

Della punctuated her pause with a long breath. "Will you tell us about the rumors?"

"Of course," Lanica replied. "That's why you're here."

But her reply was cut short by voices rising beyond the portal. Then a massive figure filled the doorway, blocking out the light. Henri searched the commons room, then rushed over. "Mr. Bruno, he says we must leave now!"

"What's the matter?"

"He says word has come, Mr. Kenneth has been arrested."

Lanica was instantly on her feet. "I warned him he was taking a foolish risk to go public at this stage. I *told* him this would happen."

"We can't stop now." Della remained planted on the bench. "We need to know—"

"You think the arrests will stop with that one man?" Lanica started moving for the exit. "They will know he sent you. Or suspect it, which is the same thing." She reached the door and turned to wave them forward. "Come or die, that is your only choice."

sixteen

Theo followed the others out of the commons hall and through the compound. Lanica rushed into her office and returned a split second later with a purse and sunglasses. She directed them toward the front entryway. Theo could see how the woman's naturally combative streak would appeal to Kenny. His brother was intently focused on the deal to the exclusion of all else. Lanica used her bullishness to combat local inertia and provide her patients with the best possible care. No wonder Kenny had offered her funding. Or that this doctor chose to trust Kenny with her secrets.

As soon as Lanica appeared, the soldiers lolling about the truck went through a remarkable transformation. A few of them actually snapped to attention. Almost all of them broke into broad smiles. She greeted the officer respectfully. When she made her request, the officer responded with a crisp salute before opening the passenger door. She refused politely, indicating that she wanted to ride in the back with the others.

Once they were under way, Lanica said, "The rumors started surfacing about eleven months ago. Clinicians up and down the western coastline heard of villages perishing from illnesses that made no sense. One person dying of a chest cold or a cut finger or a virulent skin rash, of course. But entire towns?"

Their return through the main market was markedly different. Women spotted the doctor and raised pale palms to the sky and called greetings. Children ran alongside the truck, reaching out to her. The soldiers shouted and tried to wave them away. The children laughed and yelled back and kept running. Lanica gave no sign she noticed anything at all.

She went on, "The first doctor to suggest a connection works in the Port Harcourt area. You know this place?"

Avery was leaning forward so far he risked spilling onto the truck's floor with every bump. "Nigeria, right?"

"Correct. And one of the most polluted regions on earth. Chemical runoffs from the regional oil industry have poisoned the groundwater and killed the local fishing industry. Terrible problems have arisen among the tribal populations. A clinician working with Doctors Without Borders began noticing a change among the local children. You need to understand, if you get beyond the compounds connecting the oil fields to the port, the road system is dreadful. Many tribal communities are cut off through the entire rainy season. But last year, when the transport links became reconnected, the returning doctors noticed that local kids were closer to normal weight, their energy was excellent, and their skin and eyes indicated a new high-protein diet. A month or so later, the entire village was dead."

They turned onto a main highway that took them past the president's palace, a luxurious compound that was a world away from the market's clamor. Blooming trees lined the central garden.

The truck accelerated into the passing lane, and Lanica raised her voice to be heard. "The doctor interviewed neighboring villages, all of whom showed the same positive indications. Especially the children. The village elders spoke of how the fishermen from the lost village had brought in a new harvest. That was how they described it. A harvest from the sea."

Avery nodded. "Then they died too."

"No," Lanica replied. "Those villages remained healthy. The doctors warned them not to eat the seaweed. The villagers ignored the doctors. Their children kept getting stronger. Deaths actually declined."

"I don't understand."

Lanica shrugged. "I can only tell you what I know. When the doctors returned a month later, the village elders complained that the seaweed was no more. The children cried at night from hunger. The doctors found the first signs of malnutrition. But nothing more. No deaths. No strange illnesses. Nothing."

Della asked, "What does Kenneth think happened?"

Lanica grimaced. "Now we're moving into rumors and conjecture."

"It has to be more than that," Theo objected. "He didn't dive headlong into this simply because of suspicions."

The truck slowed and halted by a military checkpoint. Up ahead, the Bissau airport stood at the center of a broad dusty plain. A few cars and trucks dotted the empty parking area. On the terminal's other side, three planes stood silent in the wavering heat. In the distance, a jet's engines began whining to life.

The officer stepped down from the truck and exchanged salutes with the guards. All of them turned toward Lanica. She in turn exchanged melodious greetings, then turned back and continued more quietly, "All along the western Africa coast, people are speaking of this Lupa. The seaweed arrives almost overnight. Within a week it has grown so thick that a child can walk across it. Then it turns a brilliant red color. The entire sea appears like a flower. The stench is acrid and so strong it will burn the eyes. A few days later, the smell dissipates. A while after that, the seaweed begins to split into patches. In a matter of weeks, it melts away."

Avery said, "That level of regional knowledge suggests the growth has happened before this season."

"Kenneth made the same assumption, and I agree."

"So the seaweed appeared years before the deaths began?"

"Perhaps. Yes, perhaps. We have started gathering formal data. I should know more soon. All I can say at this point is, the fatalities only started this year." Lanica gestured toward the terminal. "Now, inside, all of you. Before it's too late."

The airport terminal was a throwback to an era of oppressive regimes and closed borders and fear. The terminal building was rimmed by a hurricane fence with razor wire coiled along its top. The entrance walk was bordered by two sandbagged military positions. Sharp-eyed troops checked their passports and spoke with the officer who had accompanied them from the clinic. They were then waved through with a contemptuous gesture. More soldiers patrolled the terminal's front veranda, with still more inside the building. All of them armed, alert, and quietly hostile.

Bruno and two of his team were standing just inside the entryway. He greeted them all with handshakes and shoulder pats intended for the watching troops. The people waiting for flights were mostly silent. The airline employees and airport staff behaved stoically and did their best to pretend the soldiers were not present. Lanica led them to the Air Portugal desk, where a senior clerk spotted the doctor and revealed the terminal's only smile. They shook hands and talked in low tones for a few moments before Lanica turned and said, "Give the man your passports. You have money?"

"I do," Bruno said.

"Cash is best. The plane leaves in less than an hour, and getting a credit card approval at such short notice—"

"I have American dollars," Bruno assured her. "How much do you need?"

Lanica and the clerk shifted over to where he could work the computer. As he typed, Lanica said, "This is Carlos. His daughter is diabetic. I have helped care for her."

"Dr. Lanica saved my daughter's life," Carlos said in heavily accented English. "You have luggage?"

Bruno handed Theo a backpack. "Everything was misplaced except for this."

Carlos showed no surprise at the news. "I have only one first-class seat."

"No," Theo said. "We all need to sit together."

"Three one-way economy tickets to Lisbon will cost four thousand two hundred US dollars."

Theo thought the amount was absurdly high.

But Bruno made no protest as he opened his belt pouch. Henri stepped in to shield Bruno and the money while he counted. “Here’s four thousand five hundred.”

“That is not necessary,” Carlos replied.

“We would all be grateful if you would accept,” Lanica said.

“Doctor, after all you have done for me and my family, I could not possibly—”

“Take the money,” she said. “For your associates. And your daughter.”

Carlos jerked a nod, pocketed the money, and handed back the passports and boarding passes. “I will personally see you to the plane.”

“We couldn’t ask for more,” Bruno replied. He handed Theo a much larger wad of bills and the ship’s satellite phone. “In case you run into problems at the other end.”

Theo pocketed both. “You’ll be compensated, yes?”

Henri laid a massive hand on Theo’s shoulder. “One thing you don’t got to worry about, man, is the boss getting paid.”

Bruno said, “I’ll phone ahead, arrange your flights back to Washington.”

Lanica pointed them away from the airline desk. “Let’s step over here. Carlos, perhaps you will join us when it is time?”

“But of course.”

Lanica held on to their passports and boarding

passes as she walked them toward the security checkpoint. "We will stand here, and the customs officials will see that you have come with guards and with local friends."

"Thank you so much for everything."

"You will give your brother a message for me?"

Theo watched her reach into her purse, extract a folded sheet of paper, and slip it into his passport. "Of course."

Lanica handed over Della's and Avery's passports but held on to his. "You must tell him I grow increasingly certain his theories are correct." She tapped one finger on his passport and the papers it now held. "The evidence is there, for anyone who wishes to look beyond self-interest and truly see. You understand what I am saying?"

"Not yet," Theo replied. "But I will soon. I hope."

"The truth they wish for you to see here in Africa is not the *real* truth. It is a *fragment*. They do not lie. They mask what they want to keep hidden behind *partial* truths."

"I'm hearing the words," Theo said. "But . . ."

She motioned with her chin toward the sunlight beyond the dusty windows. "Here we deal with one reality. We identify an illness and we treat it. When we can. When the medicines are available. When we can reach patients in time, and have the resources and properly trained personnel."

Theo nodded slowly. "That is what the local leaders want us to focus on. That things are getting better, and there is hope for the future."

"Correct. You have seen how busy we are, dealing with our little fragment of truth. What is more, we must remain here. Under their supervision. Being watched."

Theo glanced around the terminal. What he saw was the proximity of danger everywhere. The risk of becoming caught up in everything that loomed beyond the checkpoints and the razor wire and the fear that stained every face. "I understand."

"Understand this. In your search for the hidden reality, start by asking why your brother was arrested. Why he came looking for your help." She handed over his passport. "Tell your brother that his friends on the front line all hope and pray he survives."

seventeen

The Air Portugal plane to Lisbon was a vintage DC-9 that smelled very musty. The economy seats were narrow and did not have enough legroom. They sat midway back, filling the middle row. Theo took the center seat. He shared a steadying breath with Della and Avery as the plane lifted off the ground.

An hour later they were served coffee and stale sandwiches. When the stewardess took their trays away, Theo asked Avery, "You mind telling me how you got involved in all this?"

"How far back do you want me to go?"

"We have time now," Theo replied. "We might not later. Start at the beginning."

Avery's motions became slow, deliberate. "I can't remember not being interested in biology. I've always been fascinated by the mechanics of life. When I got to university, I met a professor who felt the same way. She's dead now."

Theo felt Della shift forward on his other side. Theo said, "You clicked."

"She became my thesis advisor, I worked with her for three years, and when her health forced her into retirement, I took over her lab." Avery looked around him. "If only I'd known then what I know now . . ."

Della leaned closer still. “This field trip only makes your decisions all the more right.”

Avery smiled. “Now you sound like my wife.”

“I look forward to meeting her,” Della said.

“When I told Claudia about what had happened on this trip and that I wanted to come home, she told me to consider all this through the lens of the greater good.”

Della said, “Wow.”

“All the children who are waiting for me to help them. All the people who can’t help themselves.” Avery shook his head. “How do you argue with that?”

“I’m glad you didn’t,” Theo said. “For all our sakes.”

Avery was silent for a time. Then, “Everybody in my field talks about being on the cutting edge. All the prizes and the recognition go there.”

Theo nodded. He heard the same words at every academic conference he attended. “Academic fields are changing fast.”

“When I was an undergraduate, it was all about microbiology. By the time I started my doctorate, it had shifted to the molecular level. Now it’s genetics and proteomics.”

“And getting more specialized all the time.”

“Right. Brain function, cellular differentiation, on and on. Thousands of new questions and problems we didn’t even know existed five years ago.” Avery picked at a crack in his armrest. “I still love microbiology. Even though the field is rapidly becoming sidelined. I told myself I didn't mind the second-rate lab. Or how I had to wait in line for my turn at the new equipment. Or scrambling for scraps when it came to funding."

Della said, "Then Kenneth Bishop showed up."

"We met at a conference. Second rate, of course, because the world had moved on and I hadn't. But he claimed he was there *because* of my studies." Avery stared at the seat back just inches from his face. "Your brother has an amazing mind. Oh, I'd heard all the stories about him and the opioids. I was warned a dozen times to stay away, to turn down the offer, keep my tenured position. You know what? There was a lot of jealousy behind their concern. And even to those who really were worried about me, my answer was the same. I didn't care then, and I don't care now."

Theo asked, "What did he say that convinced you?"

"He called vaccines the ugly stepsister of the pharmaceutical industry. He bragged about how he had bought the company for a song."

"I heard him use those exact words," Della said. "It was the first corporate gathering I attended as an employee. He described how the other prospective buyers treated the entire industry as a has-been. But Kenneth Bishop saw vaccines as the start of a whole new empire."

Avery looked at Della and smiled. "He gave me the same spiel."

"Only it wasn't a spiel, was it?"

"Most of these other companies Kenneth spoke about, they see vaccines as no longer sexy. All the *real* work has already been done."

Della nodded. "Like your field, or so they thought. But something changed, didn't it?"

"*Everything* changed," Avery replied. "Superbugs began rampaging through hospitals, untreatable with our latest and strongest antibiotics. As Kenneth said, vaccines became the only bullet left in an otherwise empty gun."

"Problem is, you only make a few pennies on each vaccine," Della said.

"True, but you can sell millions of them," Avery said. "Billions, in some cases."

"Right. A billion pennies is a lot of money."

Avery smiled. "Kenneth Bishop said that as well." He closed his eyes then, shutting out the world and ending the conversation.

Theo thought the scientist looked exhausted. He supposed they all did. He turned to Della, intending to tell her how great it was to feel so in sync with a beautiful woman. He wanted to tell her a lot of things. But she had leaned back and closed her eyes too. Della sighed once, a soft release of tension and breath. She appeared to have drifted off.

All Theo saw of the Lisbon airport was a long corridor. They were met planeside by a pretty lady in a blue Delta uniform, who personally led them to the jet bound for D.C. The looks given them by other passengers when they boarded suggested the plane had been held up just for them. As soon as they were seated, Theo turned on the satellite phone, asked Della for the number, and called his brother. The phone rang and rang. Finally, an automated voice came on the line and said that the mailbox was full. The line went dead. Theo sat holding the phone, wondering. Even if Kenny was still in police custody, surely somebody would be monitoring his phone, Amelia or his assistant or the lawyer. Somebody. The fact that no one answered was somehow more troubling than hearing Kenny had been arrested.

Delta's first-class mini-cubicles made conversation difficult, and he was exhausted. Theo ate an excellent meal, then slept the rest of the flight. He woke when the attendant touched his shoulder and said they were arriving.

Soon as they landed, Theo used the satellite phone and again called his brother. This time it was answered on the first ring. A young woman said, "Kenneth Bishop's phone."

"Hi, this is Theo, his brother. I was wondering if—"

"Oh, yes, Dr. Bishop. We were hoping you would call. Just one moment, please."

"Wait, I really . . ." He went quiet. The woman was already gone.

The phone clicked several times, then a familiar male voice said, "Preston Borders here. Dr. Bishop?"

"Yes."

"Where are you now?"

"We just landed in Washington. How is my brother?"

"That is not the most pressing issue. The authorities seek to implicate you in what they claim are his activities in the illegal drug trade."

"That's ridiculous. I haven't seen my brother in years."

"They are investigating Mr. Kenneth's financial status and can clearly see that you are currently operating under the guise of his company." There was a faint buzzing noise. "Hold just a moment, please. I have another call."

Theo looked up to see Della watching him over the divide. "What's up?"

"I'm not sure. It sounds like—"

"Dr. Bishop, are you there?"

"Still here." He held up an index finger to Della. Wait.

"We have been monitoring your whereabouts since learning of this development. My associate has just arrived at Dulles. Marilyn Riles is a specialist in criminal litigation. Might I suggest you formally retain her services?"

Theo spotted three officials in blue FBI

windbreakers appear in the plane's doorway. "Yes. I agree."

"Splendid. Might I suggest you extend that representation to include your two companions?"

"Absolutely. Federal agents have just shown up."

"Instruct your associates they are to say nothing unless your attorney is present. Good luck, Dr. Bishop. I hope we can speak again very soon."

Theo had survived several near-death experiences. Hiking in winter had brought him very close to razor-edge danger. He had been trapped once in the High Sierras by a freak snowstorm. Another time, six of them had been attacked by a bear, which they learned later had been wounded by a hunter too drunk to track down his prey and finish what he'd started. Every such high-threat event had drawn from Theo new discoveries about his own character. Theo knew now that he responded to such elemental moments, when life and death were separated by the thinnest of veils, with calm. Just like now.

He sat in the first-class seat and felt the world drift into a fog of his own making. He knew Avery and Della were speaking to him, wanting to know what was happening. But first he had to plan. When he blinked and refocused, Theo felt as though he had been away for hours. But he knew it was probably less than a minute.

He kept his voice low. "Both of you be quiet, lean in, and listen."

Something in his tone silenced them.

He went on, "We only have a second. No talking back. No arguments. Our safety and our success rely upon your getting this right. To anyone who wants to know where we've been, tell them this and nothing more. Kenny sent us to Guinea-Bissau to inspect his hospital. Della, he wanted you to develop a story. Avery, there were infections and possible vaccine issues he wanted you to check out. Demand legal representation. Help is on the way. That's it. Here they come."

They were still frozen in place when the blue-jacketed agents stopped in front of them and said, "Della Haverty, Theodore Bishop, Avery Madison?"

"Yes," Theo replied.

"You're coming with us."

Avery asked, "What about our things?"

"An agent will see to them." The agent pulled plastic zip-tie handcuffs from his pocket. "Stand up and turn around."

eighteen

They were cuffed and escorted off the plane with one agent on lead and three more gripping their left elbows. The agents guided them up the gangway, past all the wide-eyed airport staff with their wheelchairs and manifests. Another agent sat behind the wheel of an electric cart just inside the terminal entrance. Avery blinked and swallowed nervously and stayed silent. The ride was endless. Theo found the stares that tracked them only mildly distressing. He was mostly concerned about his two friends.

They were taken through a Personnel Only gate and down a series of ramps, deep into Dulles Airport's underbelly. They halted before a glass wall adorned with a number of shields—FBI, Homeland, DEA, Airport Security, Customs and Border Control. The agents took hold of their elbows and walked them through the bullpen. A dark-skinned woman with eyes like broken shards of obsidian emerged from her office. "Which one of you is Theodore Bishop?"

"That's me."

"Put him in one," she said. "Two and three are occupied. The scientist can cool his heels in four. The PR lady here can sit her turn on the bench."

"Yes, ma'am."

Her face was creased by two deep furrows that ran from the crest of her nose down either cheek. When she squinted at Theo, the folds deepened like ancient scars. "Look, Theodore . . . or should I call you Theo?"

"Lawyer."

"It would be in your best interests not to mention those of your pals—"

"I am publicly demanding my constitutional right to have my attorney present during questioning."

She crossed her arms. "I think you're a troublemaker. I don't like troublemakers."

"And I think you're a bully," Theo replied. "Know what I think of bullies?"

She glared at him for a long moment, then jerked her head at the rear corridor and returned to her office.

The agents led Theo down the hall and into a windowless box with painted concrete walls and two metal chairs. They cuffed his wrist to a narrow table and left without saying a word.

Theo found himself remarkably untroubled by his incarceration. The hard surfaces and windowless confines and the agents' stern expressions all helped to push away the jet-lag fog. Everything he saw, everywhere he looked, all told him the same thing. He had one chance to get this right.

Half an hour passed. Theo could hear voices

pass up and down the corridor. At last the door opened, and a man stepped inside. "Well, hello there."

The newcomer could not have been more different from the other agents. For one thing, he was smiling. The man was tall and fortyish and wore an expensive-looking sports jacket, knit silk tie, and pleated gabardine trousers. He walked to the corner and unplugged the camera attached to the point where the walls met the ceiling. "Name's Martin Thorpe. Nice to make your acquaintance, Dr. Bishop. Sorry about all this rigmarole."

Theo had no idea what to say, so he remained silent.

"For the record, your incarceration has nothing to do with me." He looked like an aging version of one of Theo's students, all dressed up to run for class president. Crystal-clear gray eyes, cornhusker blond hair, confident smile. He crossed his arms and leaned against the wall. "I'm just using it as an opportunity to introduce myself."

"Any particular reason why I should believe you?"

"Absolutely." He straightened, leaned across the table, and slipped a card into Theo's pocket. "Because I was never here."

He walked back over and started to plug the cord back into the camera, then paused and added, "When you get your act together, if you need something, give me a call. I might be able to help."

Another half hour passed. Or it could have been a couple of days. The minutes seemed endless. Theo went through several switchbacks. One moment he was certain he had mentally covered all the bases he could at this point. The next, the walls began closing in. The pressure came from all the unseen obstacles, every danger he had not yet identified. He also had no answer to how he was rearranging his life around a brother he did not know. But there was a greater sense of need here, an urgency that could not be denied. Theo believed Kenny had uncovered a hidden threat. The lives of villages, towns, whole cities were at stake. And something more. Kenny would not be involved in this if it was only a crisis in West Africa. Theo was certain his brother feared this Lupa would become a threat to America as well. The handsome young agent who came and went in a cloud of mystery had confirmed the fact. Theo's confidence that he was on the right track kept the walls from compressing him into full panic mode.

Then the lock clicked, and the hard-faced woman walked in. One of the male agents who had apprehended them on the plane entered with her. And a younger woman in a go-to suit of navy gabardine. Theo assumed she was Marilyn Riles, the trial attorney sent by Preston Borders. The last person to enter the room was by far the largest—a tall, big-boned African with eyes cold as a carbon blade. The African focused on Theo and said, "Well, well. The troublemaker himself."

The young attorney demanded, "Release my client."

The hard-faced female agent replied, "In a moment."

"Let me try and clarify the situation." Marilyn Riles was slight and young and had a voice to match. Yet something about her left Theo certain she could be hard as nails. "Unless you are pressing charges, you will release my client *now.*"

The senior agent pointed at Theo with her chin. The other agent walked over and released Theo's wrist from the table. While he did so, the female agent asked Theo, "How much do you know about your brother's illegal operations?"

"Don't answer that," Marilyn snapped.

Theo responded anyway. "Nothing at all. Including what about his business is illegal. If anything."

The woman snorted, then turned to the African and said, "He's all yours."

"If only that were true." The African revealed a feral gleam that would have suited a lion waiting in the tall grass. He wore an expensive gray suit of rough silk that glinted in the room's harsh light. He walked over and loomed above Theo. "Your brother, Dr. Bishop, seeks to profit from my continent's misery. Again."

Theo rose slowly from his chair. Not backing off an inch. "And you are?"

"Ambassador to the United States from the Organization of African States, my good sir. My mandate is to stamp out all vestiges of the colonial arrogance that has so scarred my continent."

"Was that a threat?" The young lady stepped closer to the senior agent. "Did that individual just threaten my client in your presence?"

"Of course not," the African replied. "Why would I bother to accuse or threaten this gentleman? Can we all not agree that his lily-white hands are perfectly clean?"

"Perfectly," Theo replied.

"Which is why I find it curious that your brother recently bailed out your company, pulling you back from the brink of bankruptcy. Just before he sent you off to . . . where was it exactly that you traveled to?"

Theo held his gaze. "I still didn't get your name."

"Your brother's many businesses are of the utmost interest to us, Dr. Bishop. Which means that should you involve yourself *in any way,* you too will become a person of interest."

"Threats again," the young lady snapped. "My client and I are out of here."

The African turned and walked to the door, where he said, "You really must visit West Africa again, Dr. Bishop. And do so very soon. I will personally ensure that you have the time of your life."

nineteen

At a quarter past midnight, Avery rose from his bed and went downstairs. His fatigue was an ache he felt in his bones. His body clock was so skewed, he would need weeks to recover. But far more than jet lag kept him from sleeping. Avery made himself a sandwich from the turkey Claudia had roasted for their dinner. He poured himself a glass of milk and carried the impromptu meal into his office. He sat behind his desk and set the plate and glass beside the two pages Dr. Lanica had passed to Theo.

Avery's father was an astronomer specializing in black holes. His mother had been assistant chief librarian of the Baltimore municipal system. Growing up, Avery had been spared the horrors of being a loner in a normal Baltimore school, one dominated by jocks and gangs. At nine, he had tested off the charts and enrolled in the Governor's School for the Gifted. Among the elite who attended, the school's initials, GSG, stood for Geeks and Super Geeks.

At fifteen, Avery entered Duke and graduated summa cum laude two years and one semester later. This was followed by a master's and doc and postdoc at Johns Hopkins, one of the nation's top schools for microbiology. Avery would have happily stayed put in the university labs until retirement. He would have been content to spend years investigating a new micro-bug, putting out the occasional book or article read only by other GSGs, and making his underpaid student assistants suffer.

Until the day Bishop Pharmaceuticals, world leaders in vaccines and rising stars in immunotherapy, had come calling.

Of course, there were the rumors about how Kenneth Bishop, the company's CEO, had made his fortune riding the opioid wave. Which only meant he paid far above the odds to draw in the best.

As Claudia had put it, she had no problem whatsoever with the waterfront Annapolis home, his and her Lexus SUVs, stock options, and the private school for their kids.

Of course, nobody at Bishop Pharma had mentioned the downside.

Which was, getting a midnight phone call from the man himself. Kenneth Bishop. Telling Avery to leave his lab and his wife and his two daughters. Not asking. Ordering. As in, leave in two hours.

Leading him to this point. Sitting at his desk, staring at two pages of data, with millions of lives hanging in the balance.

The standing lamp between his chair and the side window formed an island of illumination amid the dark. When they first bought the Annapolis home, Avery had argued with his wife over her purchasing the antique mahogany desk, the brass chandelier with matching lamps, the heavy leather sofa set, the artwork. He had complained that he was a scientist, and a scientist didn't fit inside an Englishman's club. But Claudia had insisted, and now Avery loved every aspect of her choices. The home office was just that, part of their home. A haven away from the lab's stresses. Or so it had remained, until now.

He stared at Dr. Lanica's two sheets of paper, but what he saw was how these events had completely altered his world.

When he had joined Bishop Pharma, Avery had traded the carefully defined world of university research for the safe confines of a corporate lab. The troubles and distress and hardship caused by the diseases he studied were all kept at a distance. His new state-of-the-art lab remained cut off. Far more than the protective suit and gloves and lab protocol shielded him.

No longer.

Once the federal agents had released them, Theo had accompanied Avery and Della up to where the Washington attorney had a limo waiting. He had given Avery the pages from Dr. Lanica and asked what they meant. Avery had not responded then, mostly because he was exhausted and emotionally strung out from everything that had happened. But as he fell asleep, the numbers danced inside his closed eyelids, and now he was fairly certain he knew what the pages represented.

The agents had also wanted to know about the numbers. When they were dissatisfied with Theo's answer—they were part of initial research from a clinic his brother was funding—the agents had threatened to keep the pages for further analysis. The attorney had scalded them with her fury and refused to allow them to make copies. One of the agents had photographed the pages with her phone just the same. Now that he studied the sheets, Avery was not overly concerned. He doubted anyone else would understand their significance. He had always had a head for numbers. It was people that gave him so much trouble.

There were neither headings to the columns of figures, nor explanations, nor conclusions. Clearly, whoever had put this data together wanted to hide it in plain sight.

He reached over and adjusted the desk lamp. The numbers leaped up at him. The first line read:

2/10/18 4.6245 7.6331 ?/?/18 141 776 0

The first and fourth columns were clearly dates. Avery assumed the first represented the date of visual inspection. He turned to his computer and ran a search on the second and third numbers. Just as he suspected, they were latitude and longitude. The map centered on the Nigerian village of Ikot-Abasi, situated on the river delta between the oil fields and the Atlantic. It confirmed what Lanica had told them back in Bissau, that this represented the first known instance of what could possibly be . . .

An outbreak. Of a new global pandemic.

Avery rubbed his eyes. The numbers were a threat to the safe world he had made for himself. Kenneth Bishop had not sent him across the Atlantic because of a possible new outbreak thousands of miles away. Somehow Bishop had reached the conclusion that the Lupa disease was coming their way.

Avery had learned long ago to trust his gut feelings. He would spend days, weeks, sometimes years formulating such kernels into well-defined theories. Then he would take even longer designing and carrying out experiments. In very few instances, his certainty was so great that Avery carried this conviction from the first moment to the final report. Such an approach held enormous risk of bias. As a scientist, he had to be extremely careful not to design a test that would simply reveal what he wanted.

Not this time.

The fourth column had question marks in the place of month and day. Avery assumed this represented the date of outbreak. The question marks were made clear because of the seventh column. This final column remained the same on both pages.

Zero.

Avery knew this represented the number of survivors. Which meant the researchers had found it necessary to search the surrounding areas, trying to find someone who had witnessed the outbreak or heard firsthand from someone who had survived. In regions where communication was spotty and villages remained cut off for much of the year, this would have been extremely difficult.

The fifth column was where most outsiders would have been stumped.

When the SARS virus erupted, scientists working in a number of different countries came up against the fact that their national systems of medical coding made working together almost impossible. So they began building a universal medical coding system. This new classification was known only by specialists working in the field of global health. The aim was to transform descriptions of medical diagnoses and procedures into instantly recognizable numbers.

The ICD numbers 100 through 199 covered the deadliest African diseases. A cluster of thirty numbers was set aside for illnesses that had yet to be identified. The fifth number in the first line, 141, represented pertussis or whooping cough.

Avery used the number in the sixth column to confirm his analysis was correct. He searched through online Nigerian census data to determine the number of inhabitants in Ikot-Abasi and came up with 40,000. A nice round number, suggesting the census takers had not even bothered to visit the region.

He logged in to his corporate account and checked the company's online data for the whooping cough's mortality rate. This statistic was vital when dealing with most infectious diseases, because a key rating method for new vaccines was reducing the number of deaths. Pertussis had a global mortality rate of 17 out of 100.

Until now.

He turned off the desk lamp and sat staring at the room's shadows. Earlier he had checked in with his company's office and learned that officials from the FDA had been snooping around his lab, asking questions of his associates. Everyone was nervous, especially since they all knew the company's CEO had sent him off on a secret expedition. To Africa. And then Kenneth Bishop had testified before a closed Senate hearing. Three times. And now Bishop was in jail.

Avery looked down at the pages on his desk.

The numbers were indistinct in the dim light. But he did not need to see them again to know they represented a life choice. If he took this any further, it would threaten everything.

Lying next to the pages was a new cell phone. Before escorting him and Della from the terminal, Theo had purchased three phones at the gift shop and loaded them with a thousand minutes each. It would be so easy to call Theo right now and back out. Say he'd had enough, done enough, risked more than enough. Now was the time to turn away. Declare he was through, throw away the phone, and return to his safe and well-defined life.

And yet, sitting here in the dark, he knew Claudia had been right. He could not turn away. He didn't know if he had the strength to complete this quest, but he had to try. Because the threat was real. He did not need to have all the answers to know something huge loomed out there, masked in shadows, waiting to pounce. The blue-jacketed agents who had hauled them off the plane might think they knew what was going on, but they were little more than puppets being manipulated by global pressures. And if Avery took this step, he would risk being caught by these same shadowy figures. And destroyed.

That was the risk. But turning away carried an even greater danger. Knowing there was a threat on the horizon, and doing nothing, was no longer possible.

"Avery?"

He looked up to find his wife standing in the doorway. "Hi."

"Is everything all right?"

He rose to his feet and rounded the desk. "We need to talk."

twenty

Theo paid three hundred ninety dollars for a one-way, last-minute economy seat on the evening flight to Asheville. He then called Harper and detailed several next steps with his attorney and best friend. When that was completed, Theo sat for a while, cradling the phone between his hands.

Next he called his home.

The phone rang four times before a young boy answered, "Bishop residence."

"Hi. Is this Josh?"

"No, I'm Clint. Who is this?"

"This is your uncle Theo."

"Oh. Hi."

A woman's voice called from some distance, "I told you never to answer that."

"You were in the shower and it kept ringing."

There was a rustling sound, and the woman said, "Go finish your dinner. Hello?"

"Amelia, it's Theo."

There was silence, then, "Now isn't a good time."

"I understand."

"Do you? Do you *really?*"

Theo stretched out his legs and stared at his reflection in the night-darkened window. "Yes."

"I wish I could be sure of that."

"Amelia, when you talk with Kenny, tell him he was right to send me. Tell him I needed to see the hospital."

"The *hospital?*"

"Yes. In Bissau. It was absolutely vital. Even though we were almost arrested when we landed in Washington."

She went quiet a second time. "You really do understand, don't you?"

"I do. Yes."

"Then you will also understand when I say that you should never call here again."

"All right. If that's what you want."

"What I want is for all this to go away."

"But that's not happening."

She sighed. "No. It's not."

"So your biggest concern is keeping the children safe," Theo said.

She spaced out each word. "That's how it has to be."

"Of course."

"I'm grateful for the use of your home. I really am. It's lovely, but . . ."

"Don't worry, Amelia. I won't call again. Do you want my number?"

"No." Her voice was very soft. "Good-bye, Theo."

He rose to his feet, as this next conversation required him to be on full alert. Theo took the card from his pocket, the one handed to him by the man in the windowless cubicle, and placed the call.

Martin Thorpe answered with, "I was thinking you might need a little more time to land yourself in trouble."

"I'm hoping you might be able to help me avoid that," Theo replied.

"Hang on a second." There was the sound of footsteps across a hardwood floor, then a door closed. "Okay, let's hear it."

As Theo detailed what he had in mind, a trio of warning lights flashed beyond his window. They framed his reflection, illuminating the weary tension in his features. Theo hoped it was not a harbinger of bad things to come.

When he was done, Martin Thorpe remained silent for a long moment, then said, "You were right to call."

"Can you do it?"

"Probably."

"Probably doesn't cut it."

"There aren't any certainties in this business. As you should already know."

"I'm putting my life on the line here," Theo pointed out. "Not to mention the other people involved."

"I am well aware of that. Give me until tomorrow morning. If you don't hear back, it means everything is in place."

"I guess that will have to do."

"You guess right. Anything else?"

"Can I ask who you work for?"

"Absolutely."

"Will you tell me?"

"Absolutely not."

Theo grinned as he ended the call and moved to join the throng boarding his flight. It was a strange reason to be smiling. But just then he would take his humor wherever he could.

Harper was there at the airport to greet him. She hugged him tightly enough for Theo to complain, "Ow. Careful. You're handling damaged goods."

"You aren't yet, but you will be soon." She swiped at his shoulder. "Shame on you for not answering my calls. And texts. And emails."

"I told you. I lost my computer and phone."

"Where at?"

"Casamance. Southern Senegal."

She took hold of his arm and steered him toward the exit. "I hear a story coming."

"Not tonight," Theo replied. "I'm beat."

She drove him to the Fairview estate. Harper chatted at first, then realized Theo wasn't listening and went quiet. When they arrived, Harper entered the code to open the front gate, then drove up the winding lane to the pool house. "All the doors to this place are electronic. The code to the pool house is the same as the front gate and main residence. You sure you don't want to go sleep in the hilltop palace?"

"This place will do me just fine." Theo sat there a moment, listening to the summer night through his open window. He forced himself to focus. "Were you able to arrange the meeting for tomorrow?"

"All set for nine-thirty."

"Can you join us?"

"Of course I'll be there." She parked next to his Jeep, which she had brought up with a friend, then inspected him intently. "It was bad, wasn't it? What you saw in Africa."

"It was, yes."

"Are you glad you went?"

Glad wasn't the right word, but Theo couldn't think of a better one. So he said, "Yes."

The pool house contained a large kitchen-living-dining area, and a bedroom that overlooked the darkened lawn. Everything still smelled vaguely of fresh paint and cleaner. His boxes had been piled against a wall, almost blocking the window. Theo stumbled through the bedroom, shedding clothes as he walked. He took a long shower, half asleep under the spray. Then he dried off and set his phone's alarm and fell into bed and was gone.

When his phone chimed at 5:30 a.m., Theo had difficulty remembering where he was. Harper had thoughtfully set out his coffeemaker, a bag of ground Starbucks, and a mug. While the coffee brewed he sifted through the boxes until he found a jacket and shirt and matching trousers, a tie and pair of loafers. He packed these into the shopping bag that had formerly held his coffee, then dressed in jeans and a sweatshirt and the same canvas hiking boots he'd been wearing since forever. He shaved carefully, finished his mug of coffee, and left carrying the bag and his phone.

Theo's actual home was the last property on a dead-end road overlooking Beaver Lake. Asheville's hilly terrain meant few roads ran straight. Theo's lane was no exception. His property was bordered by steep forest on two sides.

Hunters loved this time of day, and for good reason. Shadows shifted constantly, reforming as the light strengthened. The night animals were weary and slow on the uptake. Body clocks ticked at the day's slowest rhythm. Theo left his Jeep on Lakeshore Drive and hiked a trail the neighborhood kids had shaped through thick brush. He was breathing hard by the time he made the rise above his home. He crouched at the base of a blooming dogwood and scouted. He assumed there was security in place, probably with regular foot patrols around his property. Then he spotted what he was looking for. A shadow by his home's rear corner shifted slightly. As quietly as he could, Theo threaded his way down the ridge.

When Theo reached the rusting fence marking the back of his property, he coughed. Again. Then he took his time climbing over. And when he straightened, he felt something cold and hard press against his temple.

A man's voice whispered, "Are you armed?"

"No."

"Place your hands on the fence. Step back, lean forward, and put your weight on your arms. Okay." There was a *click,* then, "We've got an intruder by the rear perimeter."

Ninety seconds passed before a second voice asked, "You search him?"

"Waiting for you."

Brisk hands gave him a thorough pat-down. "Okay, let's have it."

"My name is Theo Bishop," he replied, "and I hope you've been expecting me."

twenty-one

Ten more minutes passed. The sentries let Theo stand upright again but ordered him to keep his hands where they could be seen. Finally, the guard touched his ear, lifted his wrist to his mouth, and said, "Copy." He slipped his gun back into its holster. "All right, let's go."

Theo had no idea what it would be like to see Amelia after all these years. He expected himself to be nervous. But as they crossed the rear lawn and climbed the stairs, he could not say he felt much of anything. Perhaps the travel fatigue carried its own version of emotional Novocain.

Another guard was stationed by the kitchen door. He opened it and motioned Theo inside.

"Leave us alone, please." Amelia walked over and hugged him. Tightly. "I'm so glad you came."

She seated him at the kitchen table, planted a mug of hot coffee in front of him, and went back to preparing a large breakfast. Waffle mix for her two boys, a large skillet frittata for Theo and the sentries. "I can't order the boys to ignore the guards. It's hard enough to explain how we need to be careful what we say on the phone. I try to make them understand the guards are like temporary friends. They're here to help us until Daddy gets back."

Amelia was much like he remembered, a trim woman with dark honey blond hair and eyes like an emerald rain forest. She wore an oversized Demon Deacons sweatshirt and jeans that suited her long legs. When everything was ready to go on the stove, she refilled her own mug and joined him at the table. "You look good, Theo."

"I was just thinking the same about you."

"We don't have much time before the boys wake up. How much do you want to know?"

He leaned back in his chair. "Now *that* is an interesting question."

"I was worried when Kenny said he wanted to send you to Africa. But he was certain it was the right move. Now, I'm glad he did it. He needs a friend he can trust. Someone—"

"Off the grid."

"Exactly." She cocked her head to one side. "You've figured out a lot of this already, haven't you?"

"Some. Will you tell me what happened to my brother? I mean, the changes he's been through, they're . . ."

"I know what you mean." She sipped from her mug. "That's the one question I can't answer."

"Why is that?"

"Because Kenny asked me not to tell you. He

said either you saw the answer in him, or the answer wasn't real enough."

"That doesn't make sense."

"We can argue about this or we can talk about the crisis issue. But when the kids show up, this conversation is over. I don't want you to mention any of this in front of the boys."

Theo heard steel in her voice, which he had never noticed before. Perhaps it had been there all along; perhaps she had even shown him. Here, in the light of a growing new day, he saw lines of weariness and worry radiating out from those lovely, intelligent eyes. The first strands of gray she did not bother to hide. The determination and willpower in her expression and her tone. She was her own woman. "Let's focus on Lupa."

She nodded. Satisfied. "When he started receiving concrete evidence of the outbreak, Kenny talked to as many of the frontline doctors and scientists as he could. Which was how he got wind of the opposition. At first he didn't want to believe that others would want to keep the truth hidden away. Then one of the Nigerian researchers he used as a primary resource disappeared. Kenny blames himself."

"Does he know who the opposition is?"

"No idea. But he's certain the answer to what causes Lupa is somehow linked to their determination that it all stays under wraps. . . ."

She cocked her head, listening. “The boys are getting up.”

“Quick. Tell me what he knows about the disease itself.”

“Not enough. It’s airborne. That much is certain. And one crucial element of the disease’s life cycle is tied to some change the region’s ocean is undergoing. Kenny suspects it is a new pollutant. Algae and seaweed both feed on waterborne pollution. But that is only a suspicion, nothing more. All of this has happened so fast.”

Theo heard a happy yell from upstairs, followed by the thumping of feet striking the floor. He sorted through his myriad questions, knowing his time was drawing to a close. “He has to have a reason for thinking it’s so critical. I mean—”

“I know what you mean.” She leaned forward. “What happens with the advent of summer?”

“I don’t . . .”

“Come on, Theo.” Like she was preparing one of her boys for an exam. “The ocean currents. They shift. And with the ocean currents . . .”

“Of course.” He felt himself clench with the force of realization. “Hurricanes.”

“The storms begin as westerly winds off the African coast. They blow across the Atlantic, gathering force as they move toward us. One of the most recent outbreaks was right where these currents originate.”

“So he moves you away from the Eastern

Seaboard," he said. "To your family's hometown."

"The center of America has a different weather system from the Atlantic Seaboard. The Appalachians are the starting point for the opposing winds."

He nodded. "Smart."

"Is it?" Her lines turned bitter. "I didn't want to come. We fought. For days."

"You did it for the kids."

"And for Kenny. He couldn't do what was necessary and worry about us as well."

He heard more thumping on the stairs. Amelia straightened and smoothed the concern from her features.

"Here they come. Theo, there's something you need to understand. *Kenny doesn't have any answers.* What he needed was someone he could trust, isolated from his organization, who started asking the same questions."

"That actually makes sense."

"If you convinced me that you'd reached this point, Kenny gave me two messages to pass on. First, don't try to contact him. It's too dangerous. They'll be looking for a chance to—"

Theo nodded emphatically, cutting her off. He didn't need her to stress over finishing that particular sentence. "I don't like it, but I understand."

"Nobody likes this less than me. He will

probably be released, but it will be only a brief moment of freedom. He's putting things into motion that will force their hand. Preston has watchers in place. They'll try to track backward and identify who is behind this attempt to hide the truth." She rose, opened a drawer by the sink, took out a satellite phone and an envelope and set them on the table in front of him. "Call Preston whenever you need something. A safe number to use is in that envelope. Leave a message and he'll call you back as soon as he can. Kenny's money and connections will only take you so far. But they are both there if you need them."

Theo stared at the two items placed before him, gradually digesting the fact that Kenny and now Amelia had been preparing for this moment. For when he returned from Africa and joined in their quest. "How long do we have?" he asked.

"Not long. The hurricane season started three weeks ago." She turned and showed a smile at the opening door. "Good morning, darlings. Look who's come to join us for breakfast."

twenty-two

Until it was swallowed by the University of North Carolina system, the region's finest school had been known as Appalachian State. The original buildings dated from when the town had served as the granite and marble capital of the Carolinas. Tombstones and building façades throughout the Southeast were sourced through Asheville suppliers. Since becoming part of the UNC system, all the central buildings had been renovated inside and out. They gleamed their welcome as Theo drove to the gym.

While he changed into his suit in the faculty locker room, Theo reflected on his time with Amelia. There was a clear sense of change in the stale gym air. Her path and his had reconnected, and they were forging a new relationship. Allies in something greater. Bonded together by her husband, the brother Theo needed to get to know. If they still had time.

Amelia and Kenny's two boys were a treasure. They had been very quiet at first, two sleepy fellows aged seven and five. Amelia nurtured them with the steady strength of a woman made to be a good mother. When breakfast was almost ready, she had called in the guards. Two had come, two more had stayed on duty. The pair had joined hands with Theo and the family and bowed their heads to pray. The little boys had prayed first and last, as was clearly their practice. They prayed for the meal and the day and their father. Theo had no idea what the two security agents thought of all this, beyond knowing that if they sat at Amelia's table, they were obliged to join in this moment.

Nor could Theo say for certain how he felt about this religious element to his brother's life. Church had been a component of their growing-up years, but Theo had discarded it when he started college. Going home again, his family had never discussed it. Theo had the impression his parents felt as though they had done their bit. The rest was up to him.

If Kenny had ever shown any interest in church or faith, Theo could not recall it.

The sentries ate quickly and then left, thanking Amelia as they departed. Afterward the boys opened up a little. Clint, the younger one, asked his mother, "Why are we talking to him now when you said don't talk if he calls?"

His brother, Josh, replied, "Because the bad guys are listening to our phones, doofus."

"I'm not a doofus."

Josh said to Theo, "Mom and Dad planned to stop having kids after me. Because I'm perfect. But they goofed and had little Mr. Doofus."

Clint replied, "I heard Dad say they put you together with spare parts."

"Dad thinks I'm perfect. He says that a lot."

"Daddy says they did such a bad job with you, they didn't have to worry with me. It could only get better."

"Doofus."

"Spare Parts."

Amelia took a damp kitchen towel and wiped their syrupy mouths a little harder than necessary. "There. That should clean the air around here a little bit."

"Ow!"

"Yeah, ow. A spare part might fall off if you don't watch it. Now, both of you say good-bye to your uncle and go get ready for school."

The younger one shouted a farewell over his shoulder while Josh offered his hand and asked, "Will we see you again?"

"Count on it."

Josh clearly did not believe him. "Why do you have to go?"

"Your dad needs help fighting the bad guys."

"Will you tell him to come home?"

Theo found it necessary to hug the little man. "I'm sure he's working on that just as hard as he can."

Avery's call came in while Theo was walking to the main administrative building. The scientist appeared remarkably calm for the news he had, which was that investigators from the FDA and DEA were trolling through his lab and asking uncomfortable questions of his associates. About his work and his direct connection to Kenneth Bishop. And his possible connection to the opioid industry. Enough questions to spook everyone except, apparently, Avery himself. Theo outlined what he thought their next step should be, and in response, Avery supplied him with a list of items he had been working on since dawn. As Theo scribbled down Avery's list, he saw the sunlight begin to knit itself into a clearly definable path ahead.

He was fifteen minutes early for his meeting with the university president. Harper had not arrived yet, so Theo stepped back into the hallway and used the sat phone Amelia had given him to call the Washington lawyer.

Preston Borders answered with, "Give me three minutes." The attorney returned in ninety seconds. "Am I correct in assuming this call means you and your colleagues are fully engaged?"

"To the hilt," Theo replied.

Preston sighed. "You, sir, have just brightened my morning. And this news will make your brother's day."

"How is Kenny?"

"Holding up. For a man as active as he is, incarceration is an immense burden."

"Can't you get him out?"

"I'm working on it. But federal statutes grant the authorities considerable latitude with certain types of cases. Your involvement will greatly cheer him, however. Now then. What do you need?"

Harper arrived while Theo ran through his plans. He accepted her hug and pointed Harper into the president's office. When Theo was finished, the Washington attorney replied, "I see nothing out of the ordinary here."

"Don't you need to pass this by Kenny?"

"No, sir, I do not."

"I'm about to go into a meeting with the university president. Not to mention how Avery—"

"Your brother's instructions were explicit. Once you became involved, I was to facilitate your every need."

"I haven't had time to cost it out. But we're talking about basically stripping a million dollars' worth of equipment out of Bishop Pharma and handing it over—"

"Look, Dr. Bishop . . ."

"Call me Theo."

"Thank you. Let me try and clarify your position. Mr. Kenneth is serving as the public face to what is bound to become a very brutal fight. Who the opposition actually is, we still don't know. The situation appears to be growing worse by the minute, which makes your role here absolutely vital. Whatever you need, I was given free rein to make it happen."

The only response that came to Theo's mind was, "I've never had money available like that."

"You'll get used to it. I will forward your instructions to the lab and get things moving at that end. Whenever you need cash, just let me know where to send the funds. The Bishop Trust will serve as the conduit. If the university has any questions, have them phone my office. And Theo?"

"Yes?"

"Good luck, sir. Your brother wants you to know that he has every confidence in your success."

"What you're suggesting, Dr. Bishop, is most unusual. To be frank, I'm not clear on why you feel we should even be discussing it."

Theo had very little contact with the new university president. Gloria Wyatt had been appointed nine months earlier by the UNC Board of Regents. She was a handsome woman in her late sixties, a former state secretary of commerce and retired CEO of a Research Triangle Park company. She was also a woman who clearly liked to operate her organization on a steady course. Theo's request had unsettled her. She turned to the academic dean seated beside her and asked, "What do you know of this?"

"This meeting is the first I've heard of it." Dean Andrew Knorr nodded toward Harper. "Harper Phillips is a local attorney. We've dealt with her on a number of occasions. She called me last night and requested an urgent meeting with the two of us. There was a new donor interested in our university, and the matter was extremely time sensitive. She said nothing about Theo being involved."

Andrew Knorr often served as the board of trustees' blade. He was a slender and bespectacled man who had entered academia after a career in banking. Many of Theo's colleagues despised and feared Knorr. He had little patience for petty academic squabbles. Knorr regularly axed overblown funding requests and travel budgets. Theo, on the other hand, had found Knorr both honest and fair, so long as he dealt straight with the man. Which was why he had asked for Harper to go through him in setting up this meeting. But today Knorr's scowl mirrored the president's. "Frankly, Theo, I'm very disappointed that you would waste our time with this."

Harper replied, "It would be in your and the university's best interests to allow my client to explain."

Theo pointed out, "You hire out accommodation and classrooms to summer programs every year. It's a major source of revenue."

"This is not what you're proposing, though, is

it? Instead, you want us to hand over one of the university's new science labs. In its entirety. And you won't even tell us why?" Dean Knorr shook his head. "Out of the question."

But Theo was undeterred. "My company will pay for use of the lab, just like any other summer program taking over university space."

Dean Knorr showed interest for the first time. "Such an unusual agreement would carry a considerable charge."

"My company will pay whatever is reasonable."

The president was shaking her head before Theo finished responding. But Knorr asked, "Didn't I hear that your firm is in trouble?"

Harper cleared his throat. "I can confirm that the earlier financial difficulties have been cleared up. What is more, the company is now debt free."

Knorr looked from one to the other. "Why can't your scientist do whatever it is that needs doing in his own lab?"

"I'm afraid that must remain confidential," Theo replied.

"Simply outrageous," the president said. "Frankly I've heard enough."

Yet the dean seemed reluctant to move on. "I've come to know Theo quite well. He's never been known to waste my time before."

"There's always a first occasion." The president pushed her chair away from the conference table. "If that's quite all—"

"My brother is keenly interested in seeing this project move forward," Theo said.

"Your brother being . . . ?"

"Kenneth Bishop. CEO of Bishop Pharmaceuticals."

Dean Knorr squinted. "Why have you never mentioned this relationship before?"

"Kenneth and I are not close. We've been out of touch for years."

"What precisely is his role in this matter?"

"Interested third party." Theo paused, then added, "And potential benefactor."

The president moved back closer to the table. " 'Potential' covers far too much gray area for this to be taken seriously."

Theo passed over the handwritten sheet he had drafted while speaking with Avery. "My visiting associate will require these thirty items of equipment to complete his work. He is bringing these from his corporate lab. He assures me they are all absolutely top quality. When his work is completed, they will be donated to the biology department."

The two administrators were fully engaged now. The president shifted her seat closer to Knorr and together they scanned the list.

Hot air sterilization oven, autoclave, drying oven, microbiological incubator, low temperature incubator, four sub-zero pressurized sample repositories, Plexiglas hazmat unit, electronic top-pan and analytical balances . . . on and on the list went. The longer they studied the pages, the more intent they became.

Finally, they reached the last item, a portable electron microscope.

Dean Knorr said, “The microscope alone will cost—”

“Bishop Pharma is donating the Zeiss Gemini used in my associate’s lab,” Theo cut in. “The most powerful desktop subatomic microscope on the market. It will be delivered this afternoon. Along with everything else on the list.”

The president said, “But even secondhand it must be worth—”

“One and a quarter million dollars,” Theo replied. “Do we have a deal?”

twenty-three

Della had never been in the *Washington Post*'s executive offices. She had seen them, of course. The *Post*'s new headquarters were mostly open plan, with a balcony connecting the executive suites to the massive newsroom. When Amazon's chief, Jeff Bezos, acquired the *Post*, he relocated the paper as part of his plan to reinvent it as a media and technology company. The old *Post* complex boasted over four hundred thousand square feet of usable space. The new offices on K Street were half that. Della knew many of the senior journalists despised everything the new headquarters represented. Still, she thought it suited the paper and its new vision.

Della was seated in the fourth-floor antechamber with Susan Glass, her former editor. Susan was on the phone, discussing with her husband which nanny they should hire. Della listened to the conversation and wondered what it would be like to have her life rearranged like that. One moment be senior business editor of a world-class newspaper, the next worrying about who would take care of their child when she returned to work. Giving as much or more attention to the nanny's qualifications as she would to a story that had the potential to change the world. And how to juggle the two aspects of a professional woman's life. Or three, really, because even in the midst of this rather heated discussion, Della could hear the love Susan felt for her husband and life partner. Professional woman, mother, wife. Della watched Susan smile at something her husband said and heard her say how much she loved the man.

Della found herself reflecting on her own failed love life and all those futile moves. Three years earlier, Della had become engaged. Three weeks before their wedding date, her fiancé had taken a job in Australia. And not invited her along. Della felt she had grown from the experience, though the cost had been far too high. Not that she'd been given any real choice in the matter. Or perhaps she had. Perhaps she was unable to see when a man truly deserved her love, and that she was fated to move from one failed relationship . . .

"All right, I'm done." Susan stowed away her phone. "Sorry about that."

"How do you manage?"

Susan did not need to ask what Della meant. She was a heavy woman, big-boned and strong-featured. She had played tennis for Georgetown and had wrists and forearms twice as thick as Della's. Her husband, Harry, was a civil engineer who worked for the city. "Some days I can't. I fly off the handle, I get mad at Harry for no reason, I yell at my baby daughter, I drive away everybody I love."

Della said, "It seems to me you're doing a great job."

"Today is easy. This meeting returns me to a place I love so much it hurts to be away. I lie awake some nights afraid I'll never make it back."

"I know what you mean."

"Or they'll decide Jerry is better at it than I ever will be—"

"Not a chance in the world," Della replied.

"—and they'll invite me to cover funerals for the rest of my career." Susan's smile was twisted. "Those nights are the worst."

"I have nights like that," Della said. "Too many to count."

"I love my work, I love this paper, I love this crazy capital city." Susan's gaze shifted to the opposite wall, which held photographs of all the *Post* journalists who had won Pulitzers. "But if my daughter ever declares she wants to follow in my footsteps, I'll lock her in a closet until she comes to her senses."

Della did not say what she was thinking, which was how much she wished she had a daughter to argue with. And a husband. And such worries as Susan described.

Susan started to say something, but then was cut off by the publisher's secretary saying, "They're ready for you now."

As Della rose from the sofa, something clicked inside her. She crossed the antechamber and followed Susan into the conference room, thinking that this was why she had come. So she could stand here in the doorway, look down at the three men seated there, and say to herself . . .

No more.

She could not change what had happened to her, any more than she could regain the love of a man who had not deserved her affection. She could not blame herself for past wrong decisions.

But she did have this.

The opportunity to take hold of who she was. Now. This day. And chart her course moving forward.

She smiled at words of welcome she did not hear. Something in her expression clearly disturbed Jerry, her erstwhile boss, because his face pinched with the residual anger she had come to know all too well. She heard him demand, "I still don't see why we need to be meeting about this woman at all."

For once, Della felt utterly removed from Jerry and his perpetual ire. She seated herself next to Susan, greeted the paper's editor in chief, and ignored Jerry entirely. Being here with an ally who liked her and valued her was nice. Yet the real issue was her own self-worth. This was the key. Della knew she was a good reporter and a better writer. Her work had value not measured by what happened in this room.

She had been to Africa. She had seen what was happening there. They had not. And nothing that was decided now, in this hour, would change the worth of her experiences.

Then and there, Della decided she would take the position with Theo's redefined group. She would investigate this new direction Ken Bishop was taking. When she was ready, she would write about it. And it would be a major work. Several articles that she would then develop into a book. Della felt Jerry's ire growing, met his gaze, and smiled. She was going to give Jerry and the executives here a take-it-or-leave-it offer. Whatever they decided, however they responded, would not change the reality of who she was.

Della Haverty was a writer with a major story to tell.

Susan turned to her then and smiled nervously. "Ready?"

Della rose to her feet. "Absolutely."

twenty-four

His working name was Cruz. He liked the sound of it, how it made him seem both fluid and fast. Which he was. Especially when it came to his profession. Cruz had a reputation now, gradually honed over the nine years he'd been working on his own. Well, the rep actually began two and a half months before then. At eighteen, Cruz had murdered the head of his former gang, along with the leader's brother, two uncles, and the six fat slobs who had always assumed being strong and armed made up for being stupid. Nine and a quarter years later, Cruz still thought of that as one of his finest days.

Cruz had joined their gang at twelve, running packages of drugs through the blistering Miami summer, then standing outside as a guard and baking in the shimmering heat. Gradually he worked his way up through the ranks, earning respect and the money that came with it. But never his freedom. He had simply traded one cage for another. The cage of poverty for the cage of a gang. Swearing all sorts of crazy oaths, blood for blood and all that, he knew from the first day he walked into their headquarters that he was volunteering for a life behind invisible bars. How the others didn't see that always mystified Cruz.

It was right there, painted in the tats covering their bodies and the street art smothering the walls. Anger and rage and gang-style cages. Like they couldn't imagine a life that actually freed them up. Like they were afraid of being alone.

Not Cruz.

So he waited and he grew and he got strong. He stayed off the drugs and he avoided the women who treated their men like prey, the good-time ladies who saw men as parasites to bleed dry and cast aside, the hurt and the rage tight around them as well. He wanted them. He wanted the release that the drugs and the ladies offered. His hunger was like a flame that never went out. But the desire to be free was stronger. So he made it part of his tag, what he was known for. Cruz, the man who had made a vow at twelve and still kept it. That he wouldn't rest easy, wouldn't partake of the women or the highs, wouldn't ink his skin, not until he found his father and shot him dead. Which was a lie. His mother had no idea who his father was, and Cruz had never cared. But the story bought him time, and space, and gave him the sort of rep that was just crazy enough for the gang's leaders to leave him alone. Let him live. Think he was one of them.

Until he took them out. And walked away.

The money he stole from the gang leader's safe bought him a new identity in a new place. He knew some of the survivors still sought him, the guy who dared defy their code. Cruz had learned to live with one eye always out for the unseen enemy.

Over nine long years he had developed a reputation. The lone killer who got the job done. On time, safe in and out, no trail, no mistakes. At first he'd taken any job that came his way, most of them so minor league as to be laughable. Easy hits, small game, target acquired, bang and gone. He worked only through one contact, a lawyer based in Houston who handled business for the mob there. Cruz's first hit was on the guy's ex-wife.

Gradually his rep grew, as did his rates and the complexity of the targets. All the while Cruz stayed careful, and he stayed alive. And his reputation continued to build.

Which was how he had landed in this place. Asheville, North Carolina. Just about the strangest location he'd ever known for a hit. Small and tightly compacted between rolling hills. Hard to get an angle on direction because no road ran straight. And filled with a bizarre assortment of types. There was the older moneyed crowd, in for the summer season and driving their flashy cars. And the local art scene, very big, very active, very weird. Loud, LA-style talk, lots of pretty ladies pretending they were the center of the universe, lots of guys claiming to have the world on a string. And then there were the locals. Narrow-faced hicks with very hard edges, acting like aliens in their own town. They were the ones to watch. Definitely.

Cruz was known for making it look simple, and for making every hit clean. Which all came down to planning. But this job came with a very real time pressure. And because of that, he was being paid double to take out a university professor.

Cruz had two days.

twenty-five

Theo left Harper in the president's office working out the deal memo. He and the dean headed to the biology department. The new building was compact and relatively well equipped. UNC Asheville was in the middle of a major development program, with millions spent on new infrastructure. Even so, UNC Asheville fed into the region's reputation as a rising star in the national arts circuit. Biology held no real significance in the eyes of potential donors. All this worked to his advantage, as far as Theo was concerned. The dean had alerted the department head, who greeted Theo with a mixture of excitement and disbelief. When Theo passed on Avery's request for two postgrads to serve as lab technicians, the man actually leaped from his chair. As soon as he could politely manage, Theo trotted across the campus to his car. The day's loudest sound was the ticking clock in his head.

He sped to the airport and arrived to find Della already seated in the baggage-claim area. Della did not seem to mind the hurried and fractured manner of his greeting. Which was a good thing, because Theo's gut told him things were only going to move faster still.

Together they rushed upstairs to greet the

scientist and his family. Avery's wife was a dark-eyed woman whose calm was seemingly unfazed by her husband plucking his family out of their Annapolis home and flying them down to a city neither had ever visited before. Their two daughters were aged nine and six. They shared their mother's quiet nature and their father's intelligence. They noticed everything, smiled shyly, and made Theo desperately want them to like him.

Claudia rented a car and drove the girls to Fairview while Theo took Avery over to inspect his new lab. They arrived to find two trucks parked in front of the building's main entrance. The department chief did not actually fall into Avery's arms in gratitude for the new equipment, but Theo thought the man looked like he wanted to.

Half an hour later, Harper arrived with the approved contracts. Theo used that as an excuse to pull Avery out of the lab and into the adjoining office. He started by walking through everything they knew. Della had two reporter-style notebooks open in front of her. She nodded constantly, small motions that marked Theo's words with an almost musical cadence. Every now and then she drew another arrow and wrote another line. Never looking his way. Thinking hard while he summarized everything. Avery asked her for several sheets from her notebook and a pen. He began working on his own scrawled designs. Harper just sat and drank it all in. Her round gaze went from one to the other, watching, studying, intent. Occasionally she caught Theo's eye and mouthed a single silent word. *Wow*.

Wow indeed.

When Theo finished his recap, Avery shifted in his seat and said, "All around West Africa, modern medicine is making significant inroads."

"Dr. Lanica's clinic looked first rate to me," Della agreed.

"Not just her. You have private groups like the Gates Foundation and the Wellcome Trust who run hospitals and treatment programs."

"Not to mention religious groups funding new hospitals," Harper said. "My church is involved in three."

Theo understood where Avery was going. "These new clinics and their well-trained specialists are resistant to bullying from politicians and regional power brokers."

"Exactly. And the result is the online collective of medical specialists Dr. Lanica is involved with. They have been busy gathering evidence of a potentially dangerous new threat to the region's health." Avery unfolded a sheaf of papers and passed copies around. "This is the data Dr. Lanica handed Theo in the airport."

Avery was walking them through his analysis of Lanica's data when Theo's satellite phone chimed. When he saw the Washington attorney's number, Theo rose and stepped away. "I have to take this."

Preston greeted him with, "Your brother is scheduled to be released tomorrow at dawn. But he expects to be arrested again within a matter of hours. Mr. Kenneth has hired one of the nation's top public relations agencies. He is using them to make as much noise as possible. He wants to wake the world up to what he fears is coming."

"Same question as before," Theo said. "Who is trying to silence Kenny?"

"I am unable to determine that. It's all extremely distressing. My contacts are, shall we say, extensive." Preston Borders sounded genuinely upset. "Perhaps we'll know more by tomorrow. Mr. Kenneth hopes to fly down to see his wife. Can you meet him at the Asheville airport at seven in the morning?"

"Yes. All right."

"One other thing. We have reason to believe that a shooter has been assigned you as a target. I want to bring in more of the team Mr. Kenneth is using to keep his family safe."

"No."

"Mr. Theo, I can't stress too highly the level of risk."

Theo was tempted to explain what he had in mind. But the fewer people who knew, the less chance there was of word leaking to the wrong people. He replied, "I understand your concern, but my answer stays the same." Theo said his farewells, ended the call, turned off the phone, and stood there watching the three of them, Avery and Della and Harper. They trusted Theo to keep them safe and on the proper compass heading. Through the glass partition he could see two technicians busy arranging the lab. Theo desperately hoped he had made the right decision.

An hour later, when they arrived at Fairview for dinner, Harper and Claudia showed them around the palatial home. Theo had never been inside the main house. The group's loudest comments were saved for the underground eleven-car garage. And the bowling alley. Theo wished he could enjoy the others' astonishment, yet his concern over the risk he was putting everyone under left him mute.

It was not until they were on the back veranda, and Avery was trying not to burn the steaks on the gas cooker, that Harper nudged Theo and said, "You think maybe you could join us?"

"I'm here," Theo said.

"You're not, and you haven't been since you got off that phone call." Harper poked him again. "Now, tell us what happened."

The girls were down at poolside playing with a boat, and Claudia needed to hear this as much as anyone. So he laid out everything the lawyer had said, including the security threat, but not Theo's plans in that regard. Theo finished by telling Avery's wife, "If you think it'd be a good idea to go back to Annapolis, I'll help make it happen."

"I'm not going anywhere."

Avery's face scrunched up. "Honey—"

"Don't you *honey* me. And don't you think anything has changed." Claudia pointed toward the darkening sky. "People are dying out there. We are here to help you change things for the better."

Theo stared at the fading sunset, a quilted gold, the sort of dusk his mother used to love. His gaze dropped to watch the kids come racing up from the pool. Claudia bundled them into towels only slightly smaller than blankets and shooed them inside. He turned back to the group to find them all watching and waiting. He knew they were looking to him for direction. He could see it in the faces staring back at him—Della and Avery and Harper. All of them believing he knew what needed to happen next.

For the first time in his life, Theo envied his brother. Kenny was born to lead. Theo might have disliked his brother's direction, his endless pursuit of money and power. But something had changed in Kenny. The seismic shift had transformed him into someone willing to sacrifice his freedom in order to alert the world to a coming calamity. And yet he was still Kenny.

He could manage people, be it three friends seated on his veranda or a corporation employing hundreds. He could direct. He could maintain the confidence required to convince others he was able to see around time's corner.

Theo sighed. But Kenny wasn't here. And the past days had left Theo believing that Kenny was right. A major crisis was right there, just beyond their ability to see it.

Theo was not going to let his brother down.

twenty-six

Cruz tracked the team containing his target back from the university to the Fairview compound. He liked this location for the hit. And something more. Thirty minutes after he arrived, Cruz was certain there was a second team out there.

He came upon a series of tells, small signs a professional hunter could read. Cruz thought there were at least three on the other team, possibly as many as five. One woman. He scouted the entire perimeter but did not find them.

More curious than that was the target's own security detail.

As in, he didn't have one.

These days, all his targets were well guarded. Otherwise there was no need for someone charging his sort of prices. Not being able to identify any security was troubling. Cruz hated such confusing elements.

He used the day's remaining light to circle the compound, then slipped back to his car and drove into the gathering night. Once he was back on 74 heading west, he used his new burner phone to call his contact and ask, "Did your group send in a second team?"

The client was a man Cruz did not know. But he had been referred by the attorney who vetted all his jobs. Cruz only worked for clients who had been filtered through the Houston attorney. The client had a flat voice, neither high nor low, and finished each word with a sandpapered rasp. "Is that a joke?"

"Do I sound like a joker to you? Maybe I've been cloned off the worst of the Batman spin-offs, a total waste of Jack Nicholson's time?"

"I have no idea what you're talking about."

"Okay. Say I believe you."

"I don't care whether you believe—"

"There is a second team on the ground. And they're good."

Silence followed, then Cruz's contact said, "Please tell me you're not suffering from an attack of the heebie-jeebies."

"I don't know what those are."

"Last-minute nerves. Come on, man."

"I know what you meant. I'm telling you, I've never had them."

"So . . ."

"Somebody else wants your guy dead."

The contact grunted. Or coughed. "I would imagine a lot of people feel that way just now."

"Just so we're clear," Cruz went on, "I get full payment no matter who takes out the professor."

"Dead is dead," his contact agreed. "Anything else?"

"Just one. What should I do about this other team?"

The contact thought it over. “It would help to know who sent them. My group is supposed to be lead on this.”

Which meant asking one of the other hunters some questions. And that would require a close-order kill. “The information will cost you double.”

“Of course it will,” the contact replied. “You won’t forget the most important detail?”

“The clock is ticking,” Cruz said.

“Good hunting.”

Cruz cut the connection and reached to the floor behind his seat. He unzipped his pack and pulled out a Benchmade hunting knife with the serrated carbon-steel blade. He set it in his lap and searched the pack a second time. He did not need to take his eyes off the highway as he fit the leather strop to his left forearm. Back when he first started off, Cruz had gained a reputation for his speed and grace in the close-order kill. He unsnapped the latch, drew the knife from its sheath, and began stropping the blade. He had always found the movement relaxing. By the time he approached the Asheville turnoff, the blade was razor-sharp and Cruz had worked out his next move.

twenty-seven

Their discussion paused while Avery's girls returned and attacked their meal like two-legged carnivores. Claudia then allowed them another half hour to play by the pool with their motorized sailboat. Their cries punctuated the gathering night. Avery's steaks were near perfect. When they finished, Theo joined the others in cleaning up. The kitchen was an astonishment. Kenny's appliances all carried brand names Theo had never heard of. There were three dishwashers—one in the main kitchen area, two more in what Harper called the butler's pantry. They made coffee and carried their mugs back out to the veranda. When they were settled, Theo said to Avery, "Now tell us what you plan on doing next."

Avery had clearly been expecting the question, as his response was both instant and measured. Like he had prepped for a coming lecture. "As I said before, vaccinations have been the pharmaceutical industry's ugly stepsister. As a result, no real improvements were made to the production process for years. When your brother bought the company, his aim was to redesign the entire structure from the bottom up."

Theo liked how the night surrounded them.

It even felt as if the kids had their own role in this, reminding him that they were involved in something extremely urgent. They represented all the vulnerable people out beyond their softly lit world.

"The one part of the process over which Kenneth has no control is human trials," Avery went on. "The process is incredibly complex. And expensive. Bringing a new drug to market costs on average over a quarter of a billion dollars. More than half of this cost comes in the human-trial phase."

"It's stupid," Claudia said, "the bureaucratic nightmare they have to endure when introducing a new drug to the FDA."

Avery said, "But there's a group of us working in immunology who think a significant outbreak will change all that. One that's soon to come."

"Makes sense," Della agreed. "If millions of people are threatened, the population won't allow the bureaucrats to slow things down."

"Bishop Industries was secretly preparing for this event," Avery said. "I'm part of that group."

"You're leading it," Claudia corrected.

"Kenneth directs it."

"From his penthouse office," Claudia said. "You're his frontline general."

Theo loved how the two of them looked at each other, long and deep and brilliant enough to defy the night. Then Claudia rose and said, "Time to put the monsters to bed. Somebody take notes and tell me everything when I get back."

Avery watched his wife and daughters as he said, "Kenneth intends his company to lead a new approach to vaccinations. Strip away everything to do with the old system that slows things down. We call it 'Outbreak Response Team' or ORT. From the identification of a new disease to full production of a vaccine to eradication. Design a process that reduces the time factor. No longer taking years. Or months. But instead making it available in a matter of days, weeks at most."

Theo appreciated how he could settle back and let the others carry the discussion forward. It was his favorite part of being a teacher, offering up a concept to a group of intelligent and eager young adults and then moving into the background. Granting them room to find their own way.

Avery said, "Until recently the standard practice was to study the virus or bacteria and identify the characteristics that define the human infection. Once that was achieved, a vaccine was designed around the microbe or virus, but in a way that didn't make the patient sick. Some component of the virus or bacteria was isolated—one that didn't actually cause a serious infection. The body develops antigens, and these fight off the infection. This was referred to as a 'non-live vaccine.' Then the next time the body is exposed to the bug, the immune system is well primed. It responds immediately because the vaccine has identified the infection as an enemy."

Avery pushed himself from the chair and started pacing along the veranda's edge. His silhouette cut a moving target from the lights lining the neighboring hills. "Bishop is in the process of developing an entirely new system. We call it 'Platform Technology.' The aim is to insert the DNA protein from a disease directly into this new viral platform. We completely erase the standard practice. We take the disease, we identify the pathogens, we develop a vaccine at the genetic level, and then we attack."

Della said what Theo was thinking. "You haven't just been working on this. You've done it, haven't you?"

"The platform is basically worked up, yes. But it wasn't ready. It had to become miniaturized. Small enough to take to where the disease was spreading. Which meant building a new system for working at the genetic level. A complete functioning lab that could be brought to wherever the disease first appears. Then prepare the new antigen system and ship that back for the production process."

Theo realized, "That's what you lost in Senegal. That's what got you so upset. It wasn't the samples. It was the lab."

"Our *only* lab. It's gone. Blown up." Avery

stopped pacing and stood there watching them. Waiting.

Theo found himself caught by the scientist's unspoken message. "That's why you came, isn't it? To Asheville."

Avery smiled but remained silent. Clearly liking how Theo was there with him.

"You're down here to keep the Feds from interfering with your team building a new setup while you hunt for the germ."

"Genetic structure," Avery corrected.

"Whatever," Theo said. "Man, am I ever glad you're on board."

twenty-eight

Cruz enjoyed a leisurely dinner and arrived back at the target's residence just after ten that night. The estate's western wall fronted a steep slope covered by old-growth forest. Cruz found a broad oak with three low branches, almost like a ladder. It was set well back from the perimeter fence. Ahead of his perch and slightly to his left was a better station, a large elm whose branches formed a canopy about forty feet wide. That was the ideal location. But it was also where Cruz had earlier spotted small boot prints, probably belonging to a woman. Which was why he had ended up here, hidden among the branches of the oak. He still had not actually spotted the other shooter team. But his spider sense kept whispering to him.

Cruz had barely settled when the target and a dark-skinned woman emerged from the house. He watched in amazement as they seated themselves on the veranda. Just taking in the night, like the two of them had decided to make the job easier. The veranda was rimmed by lights set into the stones that cut the pair into tight lines and shadows. If the professor had placed a target at head height, the shot could not have been easier.

Cruz unzipped his rifle pack and extracted the Zeiss night scope. He took fifteen minutes doing a careful sweep of the perimeter. By the time he replaced the night scope, Cruz was certain the professor had no security personnel on duty.

It had been years since the last time Cruz had been sent after a target who left himself totally open. Why pay his sort of rates to take out a sitting duck? A local hitter could drive out, do this guy, and save the client a cool quarter mil.

But a job was a job.

Another woman emerged from the house and seated herself with the pair. The night was so quiet he could hear the three of them chatting up there on the veranda. He wondered if they had even bothered to turn on the alarm system. He had spotted the motion sensors during his first foray. The way they sat there, totally absorbed in whatever they were talking about, left him fairly certain they didn't have a clue.

Cruz unzipped his padded case the rest of the way and extracted the rifle. He had a dozen or more of them to pick from. But this was his preferred model for midrange jobs. The AP4 was made by Panther Arms, a compact version of the long-range .308 model. It had twice the punch of the M4, with incredible accuracy and a full-clip weight of just eleven pounds. He fitted the Leupold scope into its frame and tightened the bolts, then slipped a waxed bullet into the chamber.

There was always an exquisite intensity to the

moment before a kill. Time slowed. The world held a crystal precision so tight and intense that he could freeze-frame the bats chasing insects in the lights rimming his target. He drew out the silencer and screwed it into the rifle's snout.

Then, as he lifted the rifle to his shoulder, he heard it.

A branch cracked off to his left. Slightly farther away from the perimeter wall. Cruz froze with the rifle halfway into position. He did not search with his eyes. The shadows behind him were impenetrable.

Slowly, silently, he unbolted the Leupold and slipped it into his belt. Reaching behind him to his pack, he pulled out the night scope again. While it was possible that some night creature was on the hunt, the crack had carried the sound of heavy weight. Which meant either a bear had come down from the highlands or . . .

He heard a second distinct noise.

The dry brush to his right shuffled quietly. It was the sound of a professional moving into position. They did not have the talent or patience to shift positions as silently as Cruz. But still.

Scarcely breathing, he slipped the rifle over his shoulder. He left the night scope in place. The pack went over his other shoulder. Then he climbed down, a quick descent that landed him in a crouch at the base of the oak, his rifle up and swinging back in front of him. Cruz stayed like that, tracking in every direction for a full ten minutes. The sounds did not come again. He had to assume at least two other shooters were in position. Whoever they were, Cruz was not about to try to take them both out. The fact that they were separated by at least fifty yards meant a second tracker could attack while he was dealing with the first. Not to mention alerting the primary target.

Cruz trotted back to the fire road where he'd left his ride. He released the brake and rolled downhill a good hundred yards before starting the car.

He loathed the idea of somebody else taking out his target. But Cruz was a pro, and pros did not make decisions on the basis of pride.

Like the client said. Dead was dead.

twenty-nine

It seemed as though Theo's head had scarcely touched the pillow before he was awakened by a light tapping sound. When he did not respond, the tapping grew louder and more insistent. "Coming," he called.

Theo slipped into his trousers and drew back the door drapes. The sliding glass door overlooked a patio of reddish Mexican tiles. The pool's lights reflected off Della's worried face. Harper and Avery stood one step behind her. Theo slid the door open. "What is it?"

"Kenny's on television." Della slipped past him and grabbed the remote control next to the TV. She kept talking as she waited for the image to appear. "I was working on my story and had the television on as background noise. I do that sometimes. It reminds me of the audience I'm after . . . Here he is."

The cable news channel showed the announcer seated behind an angled desk, forming tight segments where guests now sat, all of them partially aimed at the camera. The announcer was a man in his forties with prematurely gray hair and a tight, cynical gaze. His voice was New England nasal and pushy. Theo always switched the channel as soon as he spotted the announcer's face. The man said, "We have time for one more question. Irma Shaw?"

The woman seated next to him was angry. "I'm still waiting to hear how he intends to answer for the opioid crisis he and his profiteering company helped create."

"Sounds reasonable. Kenneth, your response?"

"I've answered her questions twice now—"

"Not to my satisfaction, you haven't," she snapped.

"If I put on a hair shirt and whipped my way down the Eastern Seaboard, you still wouldn't be satisfied."

"No, but I'd be mightily pleased by the sight."

Perhaps it was Kenny's haggard image. Or the way he winced at the woman's acid tongue. But Theo found himself hurting for his brother. Kenny's appearance on the show had clearly cost him dearly. And yet there he sat, struggling to make himself heard. Kenny's voice held a ragged edge as he said, "The real question you need to be asking is, why am I here? Why haven't I hidden myself behind layers of attorneys and guards? There is only one answer to that. I have information so critical, so time sensitive that I am forced to put up with this nonsense to be granted a national audience."

"This is *hardly* nonsense."

"A new viral outbreak is growing as we speak. If we don't prepare for it, we could be facing a pandemic worse than the influenza crisis of 1918. We need—"

"And that's all we have time for tonight." The camera shifted back to the announcer. But behind him, the television audience could still see Kenny talking into a dead microphone. "Many thanks to tonight's guests, Dr. Irma Shaw and Kenneth Bishop. This is *The Midnight Hot Seat* signing off."

thirty

Cruz woke up as usual the hour before dawn. He had never needed much sleep. The habit had saved him from several dreadful ends as a kid, when his mom had hooked up with guys who scalded their awful home with danger. He had not thought of those bad times in years.

When he had first started off as a free agent, nightmares from those times had leaked through his tight armor, waking him in hard sweats. Being out on his own had been a difficult but necessary shift, and he had never regretted the move. The gang was history. If he had stayed with them, he'd either be in jail or dead by now. Going it alone was his only way forward. The early nightmares had simply been part of that shift.

Normally, Cruz rose while it was still dark, fixed a pot of green tea, and began his sunrise salute. It was a term from eastern combat techniques. Salute the sun with motions that started in calm cadence and gradually grew faster and more violent. By the time he finished, Cruz spun out webs of sweat and fury. The motions were called *katas*, stylized one-man battles. But Cruz could not do them now, and his body ached from the energy he had to keep hidden. Which was why his memories had leaked out.

The sun rose and the camp woke around him. Cruz stayed as he was, pretending to sleep. His hammock was slung between two trees just off the camp's main trail. He kept his face turned toward the people passing by, giving everyone a clear view. He had to assume the other hunters had done the job. Yet he couldn't leave the region until the kill was confirmed. Which meant establishing an alibi noted by all the passing campers. Even when his fake beard itched and his body jerked from recollections that kept pushing out like steam from a kettle shrilling to be taken off the fire.

The Rainbow Gathering was a loose-knit community. They congregated annually in remote forests around the world. The gathering lasted anywhere from a week to a month and a half. Supposedly they all shared an ideology of peace, harmony, freedom, and respect. But Cruz had visited several of them, and he knew different. The core group might feel that way, but a growing number of those who found their way to such places came for another reason entirely.

They wanted to be someone else.

For some time now, Cruz had been observing five such gatherings. He liked the anonymity of these places. Renaissance festivals were a hoot, with visitors paying fifty to a hundred dollars per day to play a medieval version of make-believe. In the end, though, Cruz had discounted them.

Renaissance festivals didn't offer overnight accommodations. And for his plan to work, he needed to be seen as staying. There for the duration, but able to slip out and do his job and be back in time for the communal breakfast. Safe.

By far the weirdest and most freewheeling of all such assemblies was Burning Man. The disadvantage as far as Cruz was concerned was its location. Each year, around twenty thousand anti-capitalists built a fake city called Black Rock, named after the desert where it was located. Black Rock was in Pershing County, Nevada, about one hundred miles northeast of Reno. Cruz was looking forward to doing a job in the casino industry, then rewarding himself with a few days of total freak-o-rama.

By comparison, the Appalachia Rainbow Gathering was tame.

The sun was finally high enough to filter through the trees to his left. Cruz stretched and yawned and rose to a seated position. Just another drifter out for a few days of relative safety and near-free food. Down the trail to his right was posted the camp's main map. Above it was a handwritten sign that read *Information and Rumor Control*. Beyond that, the trail branched off. One path ran back around a ridge nearby and eventually joined a secondary road where Cruz had hidden his rental car. Another path snaked through what was known as the Trading Circle.

Cruz had trouble not laughing every time one of the followers tried to explain what they were after: love, peace, nonviolence, environmentalism, non-consumerism, non-commercialism, volunteerism, mutual respect, consensus building, diversity. On and on the labels went. It reminded him of reading the contents off the back of a cereal box. Everything a growing body needed. Like that.

Cruz rolled up his hammock, stuffed it in his pack, and went in search of a shower and food. Using money to buy or sell anything at Rainbow Gatherings was taboo. There were also no paid organizers. Volunteers were called "focalizers." Participants were expected to contribute money, labor, material, whatever. When he emerged from the showers, Cruz dropped a bill into one of the collection boxes—"magic hats" in festival parlance—and joined the line snaking up to a smiling trio of young lovelies dishing out food. He ate in a communal huddle beneath a clump of wild dogwoods. Cruz pretended to listen and smile as the talk circulated. But his mind stayed busy going back over the previous night's events. He had never worked with a tandem crew before and he didn't like the feeling. Safety meant total control. Having a second pair of hunters involved meant added risk. Cruz hated risk of any kind. It was how he stayed alive.

He finished his meal and stretched out under the trees, using his pack as a pillow. He wore woven leather bands on one wrist, colored Brazilian wish bracelets on the other. Hiking boots, jeans, a T-shirt so faded that the band it advertised could not be identified. Cruz ran one hand down the length of his fake beard. He counted the strokes. When it reached a hundred, he figured he had wasted enough time. He rose and sketched an easy farewell to the others.

He shouldered his pack and hiked around the ridge and down the secondary road. A mile south, two farm tracks opened up to either side. Cruz scouted the empty asphalt, then slipped into the bushes. The trail ran through the forest for a hundred yards, then opened into a pasture holding two horses and his car. He loaded up and eased back down the trail. Ten yards from the road, he got out and scoped the road. He returned to the car and drove forward, all windows open for any sound. He heard nothing but birdsong and the wind whispering through the pines. He tore off his beard and stowed it in his pack, then turned onto the road and headed toward town. Searching for a place with Wi-Fi so he could get the good news.

thirty-one

A dawn mist clung tightly to Asheville when Theo set out the next morning. He avoided the interstate. This time of year it was filled with tourists impatient to reach the Appalachian trailheads, and wealthy summer residents who drove like they were bulletproof. Theo threaded his way through sleepy city streets and made good time.

The fog began to burn off just as Theo approached the airport. The private entrance was separated from the main terminal by parking lots and the administration building. Asheville had recently become a trendy new summer scene. The high season saw as many as one hundred private jets take off and land each weekend. But early midweek the terminal was empty save for airport personnel and two dark-suited security guards. A square-faced woman with big shoulders and large hands approached him. "Good morning, Dr. Bishop. This way, please."

She led him through the building and over to where a bored NSA officer checked his ID and cleared him through security. They exited the building and walked past two needle-shaped jets, over to where another trio of security surrounded a Gulfstream. Theo was heading for the stairs when he heard a familiar voice and stopped. The security agent started to say something, but Theo showed her a flat upraised hand and shifted over to where he stood beside the stairs, up close to the jet's body. He could hear what was being said inside the plane. So could the security. The two voices were that loud.

Amelia shouted, "I want this to *stop.* I want you to come *home.*"

"I want that too," Kenny said. "Very much so."

"Then do what they say."

"Honey, you know I can't."

"I know I *hate* this."

"So do I. But it's necessary."

"You don't have to be the . . . whatever you called it."

"Alarm beacon," Kenny said.

"I hate that concept most of all."

"Somebody needs to stand on the hilltop and shout the warning. This time it happens to be me."

"But *why?*"

"You know the answer to that." Kenny sounded both resigned and exhausted. But he was also very certain. "You were the one who brought me—"

"Don't you *dare* throw that in my face."

"I'm not doing anything of the sort, and you know it."

Amelia was quiet for a long moment. Theo

suspected she was weeping. Then, "This hurts me. So much."

"There is nothing I want less than to hurt you."

"But you are, Kenny. Me and the kids. You're hurting us a lot."

The security agent who had escorted Theo stepped quietly over beside him. No doubt getting out of sight from anyone who might pass in front of the jet's entryway. Theo heard his brother say, "How long did you pray for me to wake up?"

Amelia did not respond.

"Years. Decades. Then it happened. And all the walls I built came crashing down."

Amelia's sobs were audible now. "I never wanted *anything* like this to happen."

"What did you keep telling me in those awful first weeks? The Lord will restore to me the years the locusts have eaten."

"I hate that verse. And you didn't say it right."

"Close enough. And it's happened, Amelia. You know it has. The work I'm doing brings it all together. Even if I didn't feel so . . . *convicted* is the only word I can think of. Even if that hadn't happened, the utter logic of where I am, who I am, makes this—"

"Wrong. So wrong."

"Darling, I want more than anything—"

"I'm leaving now. I want you to come with me. The children need their father. I need my husband. That's what I know. That's the *only* logic that matters."

"You know I can't." Footsteps thumped down the passageway above Theo's head. "Amelia, please don't . . ."

She almost stumbled as she started down the stairway. But she kept herself erect with a two-handed grip on the railing. Two agents followed her as she stormed across the tarmac and into the terminal.

Theo remained where he was, pondering everything he had just heard. Then the agent lifted her hand so that her watch was directly in front of Theo's eyes. She tapped the watch face and murmured, "You're on."

Theo entered the jet to find his brother lowering two seats by the rear galley so as to form a pallet. The cabin smelled of old perfume and stale clothes. Kenny did not give any sign he noticed his brother's arrival. Instead, he rolled his suit jacket into a ball, lay down on the seats, and stuffed the jacket behind his head. His shirt was one big wrinkle. He raised one arm to cover his eyes, exposing an old sweat stain. So much for the luxury of private jets.

Theo asked, "Are you okay?"

"Migraine." Kenny kept his eyes covered. "I always get one when Amelia and I argue."

Theo glanced behind him and saw that the door

leading to the cockpit was shut. “Anything I can do?”

“Absolutely.” Kenny waved his free arm at the opposite table. “You need to see a video message from Lanica. Came in late last night. She said she’d be sending a second one this morning, but it hasn’t arrived.”

Theo settled into the leather seat. The laptop and a Bible were the only personal items he saw in the entire plane. Theo opened the Book. Page after page was heavily annotated, with underlined verses and tight, handwritten notes covering the top and bottom and both margins.

Theo shut the Bible and opened the computer. “I need your password.”

“AmeliaClintJosh, without spaces.”

He typed, then hit pause when Lanica’s face appeared. “Can I get you something? A cold compress, aspirin, something?”

“I took a pill. It needs a while to start working.” The free arm waved once more. “There’s fresh coffee in the galley.”

“I’m good.” Theo hit play and listened as a worried Dr. Lanica came to life.

“Kenneth, there’s been a new outbreak. The info just came through the system two hours ago. It appears to be very real.”

Theo hit pause again. “I thought she said contact like this wasn’t safe.”

“I had my techies work this out. We set up a

video conference feed to piggyback on their existing system. It's sort of dark web." The hand rose and fell limply. "Complicated."

"Can you give me access? I want Avery and Della to see this."

"Call Preston. Tell him I said to arrange it."

Theo still did not move. "I think what Amelia said makes a lot of sense."

"So do I. That's the problem."

"I like the idea of you taking yourself out of danger."

"Tough. We're not dealing with likes and dislikes this morning."

Theo had to smile. "This is the closest we've ever come to a normal conversation."

His words caused Kenny's features below the elbow to constrict. Or perhaps it was just a pain spasm from the migraine. His voice sounded raw when he said, "Play the message, Theo."

He hit play and heard Lanica explain, "The doctor who reported the new Lupa outbreak is someone I trust. He was visiting the region just south of the bay when he heard reports that the bloom had started. He immediately drove up. He says breathing has become extremely difficult. This is a new symptom. Of course, it's also the first time we've heard from someone who is actually living through the beginning of a potential outbreak."

Theo watched as Lanica shifted her computer

and held up a map showing the African coast. "This is the border region between southern Guinea-Bissau and Guinea. This green triangle is the Castanhez National Forest. Below that is the Gadamael River basin. My contact is based here, at Gadamael Port. His name is Dominique Lorecq, a GP with Doctors Without Borders. The outbreak was here, eighty miles closer to the coast, in the village of Cacine. The local chief is Dominique's friend. He called yesterday when the bloom, the Lupa, was first sighted. Within three hours, the bloom covered the entire delta—a stretch of water that's twelve miles wide here by the village. I've been in contact with my allies in the military. They're trying to find me a chopper. I will contact you as soon as I return. Which I'm told should be around nine in the morning your time."

She cut the connection without a farewell. The screen froze on her tense, worried, exhausted image. Theo stared at it a moment, then glanced at his brother. The lower half of Kenny's face looked exactly like Lanica's.

Kenny said, "The first time I went to Africa, I hated everything about it. I was part of a WHO junket, western pharma companies sending senior execs on a seventy-two-hour introduction to life on the front line. Lanica served as my escort. I flew over in Nestlé's Gulfstream, came back with Bayer. Guess what happened in between?"

Theo stared at the blank computer screen. A dark rendering of his own weary face stared back at him. "Your world got knocked off its axis."

Kenny was slow to respond. "I went out one guy. I came back another."

Theo nodded to his reflection. "I understand."

"Every night for weeks after I got back, I woke up Amelia with these nightmares. The experience I kept reliving didn't actually last more than a minute. We were in this air-conditioned convoy of Land Rovers, driving into the bush to visit a new clinic. Abbott Labs was co-financing it with someone, I forget who. We passed through a village where they held a regional market. We stopped at a crossroads. There was this kid sitting on a concrete block between two booths selling spices. He had pus in the corner of one eye, and the iris was going white. The guy next to me was a senior technician from Abbott. He said it was glaucoma, a common illness among the young in that region. The scientist might as well have been examining a lab rat, for all the concern he showed." Kenny was quiet a long moment. "I don't need to tell you what my nightmare was."

Theo shut the laptop and turned to face his brother. "You saw your own sons sitting there in the dirt."

Kenny nodded. When he spoke, it was in a voice so dull it sounded metallic. "So long as I owned the pharmaceutical group involved in opioids, I never broke the law. That was the mantra I told myself every time I looked in the mirror. I hired lawyers who specialized in walking the knife's edge of legality. I kept telling myself the money I was making excused almost anything. And then one day . . ."

Theo could have supplied any number of ways to finish that sentence. But his gaze remained held by the Book on the table before him.

"Three months after my first trip, I returned to West Africa with Amelia. We spent a week with Lanica. Three months after that, she called about another Lupa outbreak, the first she could personally confirm. Now it seems like . . ." Kenny struggled to a seated position. His features tightened from the pain of moving. "At first Amelia kept saying how I had been remade so I would be ready to do this. Now . . ."

Kenny stopped because the pilot's door opened and the uniformed officer said, "Sorry to interrupt, sir. You wanted to know when it was time to take off."

"Two minutes." Kenny got to his feet. He embraced Theo, a fierce grip that lasted a few seconds at most. When he released his brother, he slumped back down, closed his eyes, and said, "You need to call Preston and arrange for your security."

"Sorry. No."

"The danger is very real." He looked at Theo

through bloodshot eyes. "I could have Preston put guards in place without your okay."

"Please don't." Theo was tempted to explain what he had in mind but decided it was not something his brother needed to know. Plus, he was determined not to inform Preston. In case the Washington attorney's intel flowed both ways. He changed the subject with, "I am probably going to need some cash."

"Tell Preston."

"I'm talking to you. It's your money. It could be a lot, Kenny. Half a million dollars. Maybe more before we're done."

Kenny waved a casual hand. "And I'm telling you that Preston will take care of it."

"Thank you." When his brother did not respond, Theo asked, "Just this once, tell me what the rumors suggest."

The jet's engines started revving, causing Kenny to wince. "I've been searching ever since the second Lupa outbreak was reported, and nothing made it out to the global community. It obviously has to be something bigger than a national government. The Organization of African States is my first guess. They're a brutish, crafty lot."

Theo recalled the man who had confronted him in the airport's windowless chamber. "But why?"

"That's the question." Kenny had to raise his voice to be heard over the jet noise coming from the open portal. “Lanica told you about Ebola’s hit to the Ghanaian economy?”

“A quarter of their GDP. Gone. She told me.”

“Six or seven countries facing a hit that severe is a lot of impetus.”

Theo was not satisfied. Something about that entire track of reasoning left his gut unsettled.

He had become involved in a number of economic studies where established principles made sense on the surface. But Theo’s focus had remained on the unseen, the deeper issue hidden beneath what everyone else accepted at face value. Uncovering these elements was why his articles and books were regularly endorsed, why he had been offered several opportunities to leave his beloved hills and step into the academic stratosphere.

But none of that was important now. So Theo remained silent as Kenny’s security detail climbed the stairs and filed into the jet. As Theo left, Kenny called out, “Do us both a favor. Stay alive.”

thirty-two

Cruz sat in a downtown café at one of the tables lining the big front windows. He was confused. Confusion made him angry. He had been hunting answers for almost two hours. He had found none. Such uncertainty in the middle of a job meant risk that was beyond his control. Absence of control meant death stalked him in the shadows.

The café occupied one small corner of a high-ceilinged room that also included a wine bar. The place had been almost empty when he arrived earlier but now was filling up with the lunch crowd. Cruz had changed into a pale blue long-sleeve dress shirt with button-down collar, black jeans, silk jacket with a tight blue-gray weave, and lizard-skin boots polished to a mirror shine. His shoulder-length hair was pomaded and held by a silver and turquoise clasp. Normally Cruz would have taken a lot of pleasure from the looks two local lovelies were casting his way. But not today.

When his contact finally called him back, Cruz shut his laptop and turned to face the window. The café had started life as a tobacco warehouse. The walls were made of brick and pine timbers, both stained nearly black by the building's former contents. The noise level formed a perfect baffle for Cruz as he asked, "Can you check the local police log?"

"Of course. What's all that noise?"

"My cover. Check and see if there was a gunshot victim last night."

"What?"

"Out by Fairview. Sometime after eleven."

"Wait . . . You're telling me you *don't know?*"

"I was in position. The other hunters showed up."

"Why didn't you take all of them out?"

Cruz nodded to the sunlight and the passing pedestrians. He had been asking himself the same thing ever since he had not found a homicide notice on the local newspapers' websites. "They were split up. Their positions were screened by trees. I could take one clean shot. Not three."

"Did you see one of them take the shot?"

"No. I was too exposed. I left."

"You ran away."

There was nothing Cruz could say that would reduce the burn. He remained silent.

The client's contact said, "So you *assumed* they were gunners. You *assumed* the job was done."

This was the problem with being second-guessed by people who had never done a hit. "These guys are pros. Accept it or not, that's up to you. Now back to the central question. I think they were actually after a different target, and their objective was probably wounded. If there was a murder, it would have made the news by now. I need you to check the stats and tell me who was hit. And then I have to work back and determine what new safety measures—"

"I don't *need* to check the police reports. I already did that. *Twice.*"

"So . . . nothing."

"*Look,* I was told you were the *best*. The situation is now *beyond critical*. If you can't finish this *today,* I've got to make other—"

Cruz hung up. Instantly the rage rose up and threatened to consume him, something he could not let happen. Rage and confusion were for guys who got themselves killed. Survivors stayed cool, calm. They went in, did the job, and walked away. They stayed safe.

Cruz sat there facing the street and the light and the people. When his fury was back inside its tight little box, when he felt steady again and totally aware, he pushed away from the table, stood and left the café.

Ready to finish the job.

thirty-three

Della spent the first part of that morning starting on a new structure for her writing project. The ideas that had come to her in the *Post* offices were now taking concrete form. She was no longer focused on just an article, or even a series of articles. This was too huge. She had to put aside her worries and doubts. She had to begin looking at the big picture. Which meant she needed to build a structure that would support a book. And for that she needed backstory. She needed to clearly understand who these people were, and how they came to be involved with the Bishop brothers. She also needed to see this as an *evolution*. It wasn't just Kenneth Bishop who had undergone a major transition. His brother, Theo, was becoming someone else as well. It was only after she had been summarizing and outlining for a couple of hours that she could put a name as to who this new Theo Bishop might be.

A leader.

She worked while seated at the counter rimming the living room side of the kitchen. The entire downstairs was open plan and about a third the size of the *Post*'s newsroom. The counter was some pale wood topped by polished blocks of blue-veined soapstone. The color was astonishing, like a vast oyster shell. She had never been much interested in the things a lot of money might buy, mostly because she had never had any. Her parents had been contemptuous of the super rich and all the false moves their money represented. Yet despite that, Della found herself enjoying this first taste of luxury. Especially here, with Claudia feeding her two young girls, Avery working at the dining table's other end, and Harper seated four seats removed from Della, working on her own list. Theo had left much earlier to meet with his brother.

After Claudia departed with the kids, Avery asked, "Would you mind driving to Winston-Salem? I need to get to the lab, but FedEx has alerted me that crucial samples will land at the regional airport in about three hours."

It felt as though he was offering Della exactly what she needed at that point—a valid reason to step back and examine her project from a distance. "Not at all."

"Want some company?" Harper asked.

Avery explained that it was standard protocol for scientists working on new immunizations to request urgent access to tissue and blood samples. This was especially true when the outbreak under study took place in regions where the quality of local labs was questionable.

Della turned to a new page in her notebook and asked, "How do you get samples when the authorities over there want to pretend the problem doesn't exist?"

A growing number of multinational groups specializing in human trials had set up in Africa, Avery explained. Testing experimental drugs and procedures cost two-thirds less in Africa than anywhere in the West. The quality of these facilities was absolutely first rate. It had to be. Three times each year, these companies flew out FDA inspection teams at their own expense.

"I'll bet you make a fantastic teacher," Harper said.

The benefit to the host countries was substantial, Avery went on. Payment was made to every volunteer, equivalent to several years' average salary, along with a level of health care for them and their families that far exceeded anything they might otherwise obtain. Sizable payments were also made to the nation's ministry of health, and often yet another secret payment directly to the health minister.

Beyond the clinical trials, these hospitals had two additional sources of income. They offered first-rate health care to local patients, at western prices. They also supplied labs in the US with tissue and blood samples.

Harper gathered up her keys and purse. "We're leaving now."

• • •

Avery asked them to drop him off at the university lab. He needed to check the technicians' work and finish calibrating his equipment, so his team would be ready to start immediately on these samples. When they assured him it was fine, that they didn't mind the trip, Avery resumed his classroom-style explanation. Della sat in the front passenger seat with her notepad in her lap while Harper drove. Della wrote furiously, making a list of points to cover later along the pad's right margin.

Avery's first action upon determining the message embedded in Lanica's pages had been to order a variety of samples from a number of the affected regions. There was little chance of identifying the virus or bacteria causing the deaths. But this was not the first time Avery had worked in the scientific dark. Until blood and tissue could be drawn from a number of still-living infected patients, he had to search deeper. Hunting the hidden depths was where Avery excelled. Many of the tactics he used had been developed by coroners and forensic investigators working on homicide victims.

Criminal investigators were trained to look for the unseen. Murder victims rarely gave away their secrets easily. Avery had taken numerous classes with police CSI teams plus other courses developed for FBI agents. It was those specialty tactics he intended to apply here, looking beyond the illness to see if he could identify what he called the *invasive component*. There had to be something that tied all these outbreaks together. The kill zones were spread out over nine different countries, almost two thousand miles of coastland. There had to be some shared element that shifted these regions into poisonous environments.

After leaving Avery at the university, Harper merged onto the interstate and headed east. The Carolina sun seemed brighter than what Della was used to, the surrounding hills much greener. Even the traffic showed a polite gentility. Della set her notepad on the dash and turned to Harper. The brilliant light brought out a honeyed texture to her skin. She was a strong and handsome woman, with determined features softened by full lips. Harper's eyes held an ancient's quality, as though nothing could shock her. Della had the impression she could tell this woman anything. Which was why she said, "I need to explain how I ended up being a part of all this."

"That's good," Harper replied, "because I need to hear it."

Della's account of how she came to join Bishop Pharma took them all the way to the airport and through the process of signing for Avery's packages. The samples were packed in four Styrofoam containers with yellow tape warning the dry ice would last only until the time and date written a dozen times with an indelible felt-tip marker. They carried the containers to her Jeep, loaded them in the back, and headed west. Once they rejoined the highway, Della asked, "How long have you known Theo?"

"Since forever. Which is kind of strange, seeing as how he only just told me about falling for his brother's wife . . . what's her name?"

"Amelia."

"Yeah. It took a day in bankruptcy court for that little gem to come out." Harper smiled at her. "Theo was engaged. Gloria. She ran some business down in Charlotte. I don't remember what. The lady rubbed me the wrong way from day one. Very big-city, lots of bangles—she made music when she walked. But you get beyond that, and the lady struck me as being half shark. Grant opened a bottle of champagne the night Theo announced they had broken things off."

Della forced herself to smirk back. "What about you?"

Harper's smile melted away. "My man died four years ago. I'm still in recovery."

"I'm so sorry."

"Thank you, hon. Nights aren't the trial they once were. Gives me hope for the long run. Grant and Theo were close. They used to take these walks. I mean, if you were to work hard at defining how I'd least like to spend a day or a week, that was what got my boys going. Up and down the Grand Canyon in a day. Like that."

"Wow."

"But you take my man to the mall, he'd be moaning and limping before we made it across the parking lot. I'd give him the tiniest shopping bag to carry . . ." Harper clamped down hard. Breathed for a time. When she spoke again, her voice carried a rougher burr. "Whenever they took those longer trips, they'd invite me to come. Probably knowing I'd say, 'Thank you very much, but no.' Anyway, the last two they made were to hike the Rockies up around Jackson Hole. The other was nine days in the desert highlands of central Mexico. When they came back from that one, I told Grant to just drop his duffel bag in the wastebin. That or burn it in the backyard. Because there was no way I would be putting that nasty stuff in my expensive new washing machine."

The landscape gradually underwent a shift. The flatlands transitioned into rolling hills. The forest became denser, the pines stabbing the sky like living spears. Della held to her silence, giving Harper time to recover. She actually needed the space herself. Being this close to the other end of a lifetime love impacted her deeply. Finally, Harper said, "When Grant had his heart attack, Theo basically saw me through."

"He did the same for me, in a very small

way," Della confessed. "When we started off in the back of that huge plane, flying through the African night, I pretty much went to pieces. I was so freaked I didn't even know what was happening. I kept pushing and shouting at the man in charge. His name was Bruno. Just your basic mercenary. Not that I've ever met one before. Big and strong and totally unshakable. I watched them assemble their weapons and went into a very noisy meltdown. Sort of. I mean, I didn't scream or anything. At least not out loud."

Harper's smile returned, which was really why Della had spoken at all. "Theo talked you down off the ledge."

"He made me eat something. He talked about how I probably didn't want to know what they weren't telling me. He spoke about some local who had taught him to hunt." Della pressed a fist to her gut, easing the tension that had risen with the memory. "Then we landed."

"And you had made yourself a new friend."

"Somebody I knew I could trust," Della agreed. "Whatever came my way."

"Do me a favor, would you?"

Della looked over. "Of course."

"Just don't break Theo's heart. He deserves better than that."

"But . . . we're not involved."

She huffed her disbelief. "Girl, if you can't

lie better than that, I don't see how you ever got yourself hired by Bishop."

"So . . . it shows."

"Oh yeah. It does."

"Theo . . . he's amazing." Della turned back toward the highway. "My track record with men is pretty awful."

"I believe I've heard myself sing that tune once or twice. Before Grant. You open to some advice?"

"Sure."

"You got to clean off your spectacles before you can see proper."

"Excuse me?"

"What my grandmama told me after I brought Grant home the first time. I can't look at a future with my new man through eyes clouded by old mistakes. Not and give our love half a chance."

Della nodded slowly. Like she was taking it in deep. But what she felt humming down at the level of her bones and sinews were those singular words.

Her *love.* Her *new* love.

thirty-four

Cruz drove from the café straight to Fairview. He knew he could not see the house from the road, so he did not bother to slow down as he passed the estate. A quarter mile farther on, the road curved around a leveled lot with a *For Sale* sign planted by the road. He pulled in and parked next to a mound of glistening red earth, then got out and opened the trunk. He stripped off his city gear and dressed in a khaki T-shirt, cotton drawstring trousers, and lightweight running shoes. Because he was going to be climbing another tree and needed to protect his hands, he added a pair of fingerless gloves. Then he geared up—rifle with scope, serrated carbon-steel knife, and a sweet little Glock 19 with a polymer frame that reduced the loaded weight to just thirty ounces. Next he selected clips for both weapons that held expansion bullets, often referred to as explosive ammo or dumdums. But this was incorrect. A true explosive bullet had a metal casing that contained an explosive charge. They had been outlawed decades ago, were difficult to find and even harder to make.

An expansion bullet was specialized ammo designed to deform upon impact. It had a collapsible space carved into the projectile tip.

Thus the projectile broadened on impact, causing soft-tissue damage and exposing the wound to extremely hot gasses. The downside was range. The hollow cavity in the bullet could skew aim. But Cruz had to assume the other hunters were still out there. Which meant he needed to be certain his first shot was enough to put his target down permanently.

Cruz figured his earlier hide was known to the others. So this time he left the car and hiked uphill through the forest until he was looking down on the roof of the main house. He picked his way through old-growth woodland until he spotted a new hide. A giant hickory rose up to where a natural platform was formed by three interwoven branches, each one as thick as his waist. The hide was shielded from view on two sides by a massive blooming magnolia tree. The dinner-plate-sized blossoms filled the air with an overpowering fragrance.

Cruz scaled the tree and scanned the estate. His view was almost perfect. On the opposite side of the house stretched a wide graveled forecourt. Two cars were parked there. The sliding doors leading to the veranda were open, and Cruz could hear the shouts of children. He settled into position and went entirely still.

Those times Cruz reflected on past hits, he always flashed upon a single image. With this one he was fairly certain it would be the oversize blossoms and their perfume. From this day forward, he would associate the magnolia's scent with death.

Twice in the first hour, Cruz left his hide. Both times he scouted the surrounding terrain, moving with a predator's silent ease. Early after his escape from the gang's idea of loyalty and safety, Cruz had signed up for a course in stealth tactics. The course was offered by three retired Special Forces noncom officers. They intended the course for SWAT police and private security. Cruz used a fake ID and claimed to be aiming for the Chicago PD. There was a unique joy in working alongside these highly trained, highly skilled men and women. He had been tempted to sign on for a tour with the Marines. But in the end he had walked away. There was too much risk of trading one cage for another. He would stay a loner to the end.

Tracking over the same territory was one of the tactics his trainers had stressed. Shadows shifted, wind altered, light filtering through trees revealed different tells. He saw nothing the first time, but the second revealed footprints. Two different trackers, one massive male and that same small man or woman. They had drifted through the clearing behind his hide, then split up and entered the forest. Cruz lost both on a carpet of pine needles. He scaled a second tree just to be certain they were not lurking up above eye level. But the day was empty. He returned to his hide both unsettled and angry. These people were good. But he was better. And he was going to take them out.

Cruz had decided on the drive over that the second team were definitely after a different target. The footprints confirmed as much. They were not out for some midnight stroll. They were also not sloppy. To move through forested terrain and mask their trail by holding to springy pine needles suggested a high level of training. These were specialists.

Half an hour after he returned, Cruz watched as a heavyset woman drove a Lexus SUV with Maryland plates out through the estate's front gates. She had two children in the rear seat. Twenty-six minutes later, a Jeep Cherokee departed. The driver was a handsome African-American woman, with a white woman in her early thirties in the passenger seat. Cruz had been supplied with photos of the professor's team. He identified the Jeep's driver as the target's attorney. The scientist down from the Bishop main labs was seated in the rear. The white woman in the front passenger seat was prettier than her photograph, another employee of the brother's company. The target, Theo Bishop, was nowhere in sight.

With more prep time, Cruz would have fitted all

the vehicles with GPS trackers. Today, however, he was left with a difficult choice. Follow the lawyer lady's Jeep or assume the target was still in the house. The problem was, he had arrived late after thinking the job had been taken care of by the other hunters. Now, if the target had left before he arrived, Cruz risked losing his only connection to where the professor would be later.

Cruz scrambled down from the hide and hot-footed it to his rental. He tracked the Jeep until, ten minutes later, the attorney took the turnoff that led straight for the university. Soon as he was certain of their destination, Cruz wheeled about and raced back to the residence.

He knew such an estate was bound to have electronic security. But these people did not fit the house. Wealthy and powerful people made up almost all of Cruz's targets. He knew them and he knew their habits. They were cautious by nature. Leaving such a residence usually meant entering into a staged process. These people were simply too normal. The only thing they checked for was oncoming traffic. There was no surveillance, no driver, no guards. Nothing. Which left Cruz fairly certain they were sloppy when it came to the house's built-in security system.

Just in case he was wrong, Cruz donned a baseball cap and hooded sweatshirt and dark sunglasses. He pulled the hood over the cap and kept his face tilted toward the earth. He scouted the empty road, scaled the fence, and raced up the incline.

Theo Bishop lived in the pool house. Cruz knew this within ten seconds of entering the apartment. The target did not even bother to lock his door. Cruz searched the two rooms in less than a minute, then headed up to the main house. Again the place was unlocked. He knew within a dozen heartbeats that the vast home was vacant.

He spent another five minutes doing a more careful search, now looking for the ideal hideaway. If Bishop did not show up at the university lab, Cruz would return here and wait. Which meant taking out all the others as well.

Three minutes later, Cruz was back in his car and heading into town. He hoped Theo Bishop would be there at the university. Cruz had never liked shooting kids. But a job was a job. And one thing was certain. Today the target would breathe his last.

thirty-five

Kenny called when Theo was still driving back to the university. The sound of jet engines and rushing air filled the car's speakers. "Preston's just completed a transfer to your corporate account. We decided to go ahead and send you two million." Kenny sounded almost amused by the news. "He wanted to make it contingent upon your accepting a security detail. I told him to save his breath."

"I actually don't know what to say."

"He's right, just the same. You need to have guards."

"I'll think about it." That much at least was true. Theo thought about it a lot. "How's your head?"

"Flying helps. Lower air pressure reduces the swelling. I'm okay and getting better." Kenny paused, then confessed, "I'm really worried."

"About what?"

"Lanica hasn't contacted me. Preston's hunting. He can be more discreet about things like that. I tend to shove my weight around like a bull on a binge."

"What can I do?"

"I have no idea."

Theo liked the easy confession. Two friends.

No boundaries. “I could try to have Avery use the scientific back channels. He’s ordered lab samples through regional hospitals.”

“That is bound to raise red flags. Listen, Theo . . .”

“Yes?”

“Preston thinks I’ll probably be arrested again. Sometime later today is the word he’s picked up through his connections.”

The casual way Kenny spoke made the news seem even more brutal. “I’m with Amelia on this. Your attitude is *nuts*.”

Kenny’s only response was to go quiet.

Theo sighed. “So, what do you want me to do here?”

“Somebody with a lot of clout is very angry over my public announcements. They intend to shut me up. Obviously we need to know who that is.”

“I thought that was Preston’s job. He still can’t say who’s put you at the top of their enemies list?”

“No. Or why. Which is curious and worrisome both. Preston’s contacts go all the way to the very top.”

Theo felt the faint niggling of a new idea. “Then he’s asking the wrong questions to the wrong people.”

“What’s that supposed to mean?”

The answer was, Theo didn’t know. Not yet.

"I'll get back to you when I have something. In the meantime, stay out of jail."

Theo spent the rest of the drive replaying the conversation in his head. Kenny's casual indifference over returning to prison rattled Theo. Nothing about this new attitude made sense through the lens of their shared past. The brother Theo knew had been focused exclusively on winning.

His mind went back to the Bible on the airplane's table and all the markings on its pages, and from there Theo relived the prayer time at breakfast with Amelia. The woman's iron-hard resolve was on clear display when the armed guards linked hands with the family. Theo drove and mulled over Amelia's pain and fury at his brother. As he thought about their argument, he had the distinct sense that something more than what he had heard was at work. When he pulled into the bank's parking lot, it struck him that Amelia had in fact been more angry at herself. She was drawn into an impossible conflict by her situation. Praying for years, was how Kenny had put it. Praying for years only to have her prayers answered.

He entered the bank and asked to speak to the assistant manager, the woman who had been on their side through the hardest of days, who had actually shed tears when she told him the bank had decided to call their loans, thus forcing them into bankruptcy. To describe her as ecstatic over the change in their financial status did not go far enough. Theo endured her embrace, her delight, her congratulations, and then got down to business.

Theo spent almost three hours setting up new accounts. Kenny's funds came in while he was at the bank. Theo arranged for the first wire transfer, putting the next stage of his plan into motion. As he prepared to leave, Della called and said they had arrived back from Winston-Salem and were all at the lab. She asked him to stop for takeout and bring enough food for six people. Theo drove to his favorite sandwich shop, then on to the university lab building, where he found Della and Harper sharing Avery's desk.

Harper was working through a list of everything she needed to do to get their business up and running again. Della typed furiously, transcribing from her notepad into her laptop. The wall between the office and the lab was glass from the waist up. Theo could see Avery and his lab techies working the equipment, unloading Styrofoam containers, preparing lab glass. Theo unwrapped the sandwiches and passed them around. Avery waved distractedly and sent an assistant over for their meals. Theo took a turkey and avocado on whole wheat for himself and studied the others. His team. They were bonding, the two women here in the office and Avery with his postgrads. All of them hunting.

After they finished eating, Theo went next door and asked Avery if he could spare a minute. The scientist seemed reluctant but joined them nonetheless. Theo asked if he could explain what it was he sought, and why the samples were important. "None of them come from victims," Theo said. "I'm not clear on what role they might play. Seems like a lot of time and money to invest in something that doesn't really matter."

"Oh, it matters," Avery replied. "Even if there's nothing, it still helps us discount potentialities."

Theo took a long look at the scientist. A new gleam was evident in the man's eyes, a happy tension. "But it's not nothing, is it?"

"No."

"You've already found something."

Avery's smile grew broader. "I have indeed."

thirty-six

Cruz could not find a decent hide.

The UNC Asheville campus was laid out like a checkerboard. There was no center. Money had come in waves, and each new phase meant another square had been inserted alongside the others. The biology building formed the link between old and new developments. Parking lots linked the bio building to two other squares. The bio building itself had five access points, counting three alarmed fire exits. The campus was in full summer-school swing. Students and visitors drifted through the sunlight. Cruz dumped his jacket in the trunk, pulled out his shirt, and slung his backpack over one shoulder. There were a lot of other mature students moving around or settled at outdoor tables. The only difference was, his pack probably held the only loaded gun and skinning knife.

He spent an hour nursing a coffee, then shifted to a bench with a clear view of the front and side entrances. The security police circled around twice. Otherwise it was just another day in the Carolina hills. Everybody busy and happy and completely without a clue. He debated relocating back to the estate and waiting for them to come home. The campus was both very public and very crowded. But the ticking clock kept him there. Waiting.

He returned to the café, bought a blueberry muffin and second cup of coffee, and chose a table that was partly shaded from the sun.

Twenty minutes later, Theo Bishop cruised into the adjacent lot, parked, and started walking at a brisk pace toward the bio building.

Avery told them, "Criminal investigators all over the country share one rule. If the culprit to a murder is hidden, track the peripheral evidence."

"I like this already," Harper said. "Calling it murder."

"Because that's exactly what it is," Della agreed.

"Peripheral evidence," Avery repeated. He stepped up to the whiteboard by the office's side wall. He wiped fingers greasy from the takeout food down the sides of his lab coat, then uncapped a marker and wrote the two words at the top of the board.

Theo watched as the letters took form in wide blue strokes and felt something resonate inside him. The sensation was so strong he could almost hear it, a powerful harmony. *Peripheral evidence.* The energy lifted him from his chair and pushed him back so that he stood near to the office's windows, as far from the whiteboard as he could get.

Avery's smile was almost shy, like he knew what was happening to Theo and was embarrassed by the impact his words were having. "What do all these outbreaks have in common? We know there must be something. Why?" He took out the two folded pages from his pocket. "Doctors up and down the Atlantic coast of Africa have noted similar afflictions."

Della said, "The bloom."

Avery turned and wrote *Lupa* on the whiteboard. "Good. That's one."

"One hundred percent mortality," Theo said. He pulled the new phone from his jacket and texted the Washington attorney, *Any word from Lanica?* He could imagine the doctor's name fitting into an unseen cavity, like a key made for a lock he had yet to identify.

"Right," Avery said, and added another line to the whiteboard.

"No illness except for the one region," said Della. "It comes, it attacks, it vanishes."

"Good." Avery continued writing.

Theo said, "We need to check wind directions for the days surrounding the events."

"Excellent." Avery entered his lab, spoke to the technicians still lounging over their meals, and pulled another whiteboard into the office. Through the glass wall Theo saw the technicians gather up the remnants of their meals and resume working at their posts. Avery positioned the second whiteboard and wrote at the top, *Tracking assignments*.

"I can do that," Della said.

Avery handed her the two sheets. "What else?"

Theo's attention shifted when his phone buzzed with an incoming message. He read, *Still nothing.*

Theo watched as Avery wrote more words on both whiteboards. He could not bring them into focus. Instead, he felt as though the concepts were rearranging themselves, becoming part of the idea that continued to rock his internal world.

He heard Avery say, "Anything else?"

Harper asked, "What are you working on in your lab?"

"Precisely the question." Avery bent down and added another line to the first board, *Seaweed baked into bread.* He straightened and said, "Kenneth Bishop sent me down within forty-eight hours of hearing there had been another outbreak of Lupa. By the time I arrived, drying ovens up and down the beach had been shifted from fish to seaweed."

"They knew," Harper said.

"There you go."

She rose to her feet. "They *knew*. They'd heard from other places about this new stuff coming out of the . . ."

Harper stopped speaking because Avery had crossed the office a second time, entered the lab, and returned with yet another whiteboard. On this one he wrote, *Timeline*.

"Homicide investigators will spend days and days working this out," Avery said.

Theo wanted to object, say they did not have the luxury of time. But as he started to speak, his phone buzzed again. He read, *Your brother is back behind bars. Working to release him. Very difficult. OAS has entered a formal request for his extradition to Ghana. His former company had a factory in Accra.*

Avery was saying, "By the time the bloom started, the fishermen had heard from others about this incredible new source of protein, and the money they could get from the bread." He turned and looked at them. "But the illness isn't linked to either making or eating the bread. We know this how?"

"Because the people in those other places didn't get sick," Harper said. Still on her feet. Totally engaged now.

"Right. Which means two things. First, the outbreaks are airborne. And second, the life cycle is very short." He wrote on all three boards now, scribbling faster, his words harder to make out. But Theo did not care. He was no longer reading along with the others.

Instead, he walked forward, waited until Avery straightened, and said, "I have an idea."

thirty-seven

Cruz stayed where he was, seated at one of the tables outside the student coffee shop, for almost an hour after he spotted Theo Bishop entering the biology building. There was no need to track him personally now. He knew the target's entry and exit points. The man's car was parked in the lot to Cruz's left. It would be nice if Bishop delivered the sacks of food, maybe had a bite with his crew, then left. Cruz could follow him and make the hit away from the university's patrolling security and the students milling about. Maybe arrange a solitary accident. Walk in close and make sure the job was done. Then disappear into the flower crowd at the Rainbow Gathering. Drift out of sight. Bang and gone.

But the target and his group continued to astonish Cruz. He had never before been assigned a hit where the target showed such an utter disregard for security. Theo Bishop's casual manner was almost comic. Cruz had no idea what the target had become involved in. Nor did he much care. Yet whatever it was, surely the man had to know he had threatened some powerful interests. Not even some ivory-tower academic could remain totally blind to the risks. Especially when the issue he'd involved himself in was so time sensitive. It made no sense.

Cruz spotted the university cops patrolling in their little open-sided vehicles. It was the third time in less than an hour they'd made the circuit, one heavyset guy and a lady in her forties who might once have been a professional wrestler, her neck and shoulders were that developed. His spider sense told him that he was the reason for their vigilance. Cruz pretended to sip from his empty cup while slowly crumpling into a ball the waxed bag that had held his muffin. He waited another dozen breaths, just another summer student learning new meanings for the word *lazy*. He stood and approached a nearby table where the occupant had just slipped inside the coffee shop for whatever reason. Three books were piled on the tabletop. Cruz grabbed the top book and strolled away.

The rental car's lock beeped loud as an alarm. Cruz hated the vehicle and everything it represented, all the wasted time, the strangeness of this job. He wished he'd never taken the assignment. Several pedestrians turned his way, giving him that look. The one that suggested he didn't belong, and having a textbook tucked under his arm made no difference whatsoever. Cruz settled into the sun-heated seat, fired the engine, and reversed from the lot.

The one positive outcome of this whole wasted

morning was that he could be certain the second hit team was no longer around. He would have noticed. Big time. That was how he'd survived for as long as he had. By noticing.

Cruz trundled around the winding university streets, holding to the speed limit. He couldn't take the risk that he'd already been linked to the vehicle by campus security. The days when university cops were a joke belonged to a different era. Kidnappings and molestations and school shootings had changed everything. The university could not afford bad publicity. Security was crucial. They hired the best and paid them to stay focused.

Cruz found what he was looking for two streets away from the university's main entrance. It was the sort of residence a senior professor might own, or maybe a dean. Red brick, not new, two stories, built in a time of conservative houses and bow ties and cocktail parties on the back veranda. The empty drive was sheltered by massive oaks. The ground-floor windows were covered by pale drapes. Cruz pulled midway up the drive to where the first pair of trees masked him in shadow. He walked to the front door, feeling as if the day sought to trap him in a web of sunlight and heat. He rang the bell four times, then turned and walked back to his car. The house was hidden from its neighbors by hedges and more trees. The neighborhood was totally silent. He opened the trunk and changed into running shorts and a sleeveless sweatshirt. The cap and shades stayed in place. He belted on a fanny pack and filled it with a pistol, three clips, and his favorite knife. He fitted in earbuds, jammed the cable in place with the pack's zipper, and set off running.

thirty-eight

Avery stopped Theo with an upraised hand and the words, "Hold that thought."

Della had seldom seen a man so much in his element as Avery was at that moment. He stood flanked by the three whiteboards, a blue marker in one hand and a black in the other. So totally caught up in his work that he was utterly beyond the normal boundaries that defined him. The stained lab coat, the dab of mayonnaise on one cheek, the way his glasses had slid down his nose, or the perspiration dotting his forehead—none of this mattered. His voice had not risen, yet there was an energy now, a passion that dominated the room.

Avery went on, "Soon as I decoded Dr. Lanica's data, I contacted a lab I've used many times before. I gave them general coordinates. Entire regions. We needed such a large population base, because there was no telling where or even if human blood and tissue samples had been taken."

The idea struck her then. Even so, Della remained where she was. Her immobility was only partly due to Avery's excited chatter. What most captured her was Theo. He had approached the whiteboards and now seemed joined to Avery, both in thought and purpose. Two academics united by a shared quest for knowledge. At this moment, Della sensed neither of them was actually aware of the lives hanging in the balance. For them, the knowledge itself was enough.

She had never known anyone like Theo before. His strength and quiet enthusiasm seemed to expand the space his body occupied. She wanted to reach out, grip him as hard as she could, and ask the question that dominated her mind and heart whenever they were together: Would there ever be a time for them?

Then she noticed that Harper was watching. Soon as their eyes met, the dark-skinned woman smiled knowingly. Della felt her face flame crimson. She interrupted Avery with, “I need to obtain some information online. Which means spending money I don’t have.”

Theo searched through his pockets and came up with a credit card. “Go ahead.”

“Don’t you want to know what for?”

“Later.” His gaze had not shifted from Avery. “Go on.”

thirty-nine

Cruz jogged past the biology building, making a casual loop around three interconnected parking lots. Just another student defying the oppressive summer heat. The same security guards who had scouted him earlier from their small cop-mobile drove along the main road. Cruz opened the fanny pack and settled his hand on the Glock. But the guards did not even glance his way as they passed.

Cruz stopped by a water fountain that marked a point where the sidewalk circled a little patch of blooming flowers. He waited while two girls filled their water containers, then splashed his face and neck. Taking his time, his glasses pushed up on top of his head, giving his surroundings a careful inspection. Two cops on foot patrol passed the rear of the biology building where it was closest to the next building, a narrow angle of shadows that weaved with the blowing tree limbs. Cruz was especially concerned by this, because he suspected if the other team was hunting, they would have used this as their hide. But the male-female pair strolled past, chattering happily, clearly more interested in each other than the hide.

Even so, Cruz felt the spider sense crawl inside

his gut. He was missing something. He could almost feel the foe's body heat.

Avery was saying, "More than two-thirds of the tissue samples showed a very high level of potassium."

Theo felt like he should be paying stricter attention. But two things kept getting in the way. Three, actually. He could see that Della was growing very excited by what she was pulling up on her laptop. Three times now she had hit a site and coded in Theo's credit card details, then gasped at what she had found.

Added to this was how Harper kept watching him. Something she saw made her smile. And something in that smile unsettled him. He felt himself blushing and had no idea why.

Plus, he had an idea of his own. One that kept building in force. It was like a cresting wave rising in his chest. Staying quiet and showing patience had become very tough indeed.

Avery said, "There are a number of possible reasons why people will have an elevated level of potassium. But we're not talking about what a western lab would class as 'normal population' samples. These people are *poor*. And something more."

Theo started to interrupt, to tell the man to stop with the dramatics and get to the point. But Avery was smiling now. Just *loving* this.

"There is no reason why a population spread out over a thousand miles, in a cluster of different countries, all with different diets and habits, would show the same elevated potassium."

That lifted Della's head. "What, none?"

"Not one. If you examine the list of possible reasons, you can discount them all when you factor in the various incomes and nations and diets and cultures."

Harper said, "Wow."

"Exactly." Avery was beaming now, his face turned handsome by his excitement. "If I were writing up these findings for publication, I'd call this our first confirmation that we're on the right track. But *wow* will do."

forty

"I have something that might help."

Della fiddled with her laptop, fingers racing. "It would be nice if I could hook this up to the projector up there in the ceiling. But I don't see a cable."

"That's because it's Bluetooth," Harper said. She walked over to the controls mounted on the wall by the door. She pushed a button while watching the projector embedded in the ceiling. A light gleamed, and the machine gave off a little beep. "You know how to do a wireless search?"

"Yes." Della moved the arrow control. "Got it."

At the same moment the machine beeped a different tone.

"There you go." Harper touched another button. "Watch your heads, gentlemen."

Theo stepped back as a screen he had not noticed until that moment began descending in front of the whiteboards. "You never cease to amaze."

"Hey, you spend enough time talking to juries, you learn a few magic tricks." Harper resumed her seat. "It'd probably be the polite thing if you both sat yourselves down for the lady's show."

Theo wanted to interrupt, to talk, to take control. But there was such a sweetness to this moment, seeing the two ladies move in tandem. He watched as Della rose from her chair and asked Harper, "Do you mind handling the computer?"

"Girl, I've been waiting all day for somebody to give me something to do."

"Okay." Della waited until Harper replaced her in front of the monitor. Then she pointed to the screen and said, "I want to lay this out in timed sequence."

Harper breathed in sharply. "What on earth?"

"Pay attention. With each one, you go in tighter, see? That's already set up. They're laid out like cards. Start with the left one and move right."

"Got it." Harper grinned at Theo. "Gentlemen, prepare to have your socks knocked off."

Entering the biology building proved easy. Somewhere in the distance, a bell rang. It was the sort of bonging note a church might have made in some distant era. Back when the television shows were all about happy families doing happy things, the sort of stories that had made no sense to the young Cruz. Three minutes later, the two girls he had seen at the water fountain drifted past, and they were soon joined by a cluster of other students, all of them wearing bright summer clothes. Cruz did not exactly fit in with his running gear, but he wasn't out of step either.

He took off his sunglasses and settled them into the fanny pack.

Cruz kept a smile on his face as he drifted down the first-floor hallway, moving a half step slower than the others. The students piled into a classroom on his left. He continued on, checking each door without turning his head. All those he checked showed classrooms. More than half were dark. The doors without glass were most likely either offices or custodial closets. Cruz kept to his easy pace as he stepped through the far exit, where he noticed a second door leading to the basement stairs. It was alarmed and marked *No Entrance*. He took the stairs up to the second floor.

The corridor was wider on this floor. Something about the layout had his heart moving into strike mode even before he saw the first lab. He decided the halls had been designed extra wide to accommodate the type of equipment used in lab work. Observing such things came easily when approaching a kill. Afterward he would sift through his memory, segment the work, and catalog what had gone well and what needed improvement. His memories of these moments were so clear they seemed jagged, like photographic images etched into razor-edged glass.

He passed a lab where two white-coated technicians were bent over a very complex-looking apparatus. Cruz did not slow his pace. Neither of them were of any interest. The room next door was scarcely visible through the glass dividing-wall. It was almost completely dark.

But just as he moved out of range, something flashed. Cruz could not be certain whether it was from the technicians and their equipment or the dark office. Still, he kept moving. Reaching the end of the corridor, he entered the stairwell . . . and hesitated. There was nothing to suggest his target was located on this floor. Even so, the flash of light was interesting. He decided to check the top floor, then return if nothing panned out upstairs.

forty-one

Harper asked, "Start with the far left image?"

"Yes. No. Wait." Della walked over and switched off the light. With the office dark now, she said, "Okay. Show them."

Theo was rocked back in his seat by the image. It blasted him, a silent explosion. From the chair beside him, Avery let out a breath, like someone had punched him in the gut. Which was exactly how Theo felt.

"These sat photos are from the third line on Lanica's list," Della explained, calm as could be. "That was the first one to give us a precise date. This is four days before the outbreak."

"Liberia," Avery said. "Amazing."

The projector's screen was eight feet wide by six feet high. The boundaries of Della's image were an emerald green, so vivid it could have been the aerial shot of some new golf resort. Deep forest greens spilled into waters that glistened in the sunlight. A few clouds painted drifting shadows.

The idyllic photo ended there. Inside was a blooming rose of death. The entire bay was a single poisonous flower. The edges were sharply defined, a boundary that weaved into several estuaries. The color appeared extremely violent.

There was no question that this was a terrible occurrence.

“Lupa,” Theo said. The enemy now had a face.

“Takes your breath away,” Avery said.

“Kind of brings everything into focus,” Harper agreed.

“I should have thought of this before now,” Avery said.

Theo shook his head without taking his eyes off the screen. “You said it yourself. The outbreak isn’t timed to the Lupa itself.”

In response, Avery rose and approached the screen. A moment’s silent inspection, then he asked, “Can you change this to the date Lanica gave for the outbreak?”

“Harper,” Della said. “Next image.”

The image shifted to one of rich greens. The water was darker, the stain still there. But it was still just another shade, one of many.

Avery said, “Can you zoom in closer?”

Della said to Harper, “Click on the plus sign in the corner.”

The image tightened until the boundaries were lost. The surface became dotted by little water beetles, or so it seemed to Theo.

“Fishing boats,” Avery said, his nose just inches from the screen. “You know what that means.”

“They’re harvesting the seaweed,” Theo said. “They knew what to do. And when.”

“My guess is, if we go back in time, we’ll find the Lupa tides occurred before this season.”

“Only this year, something changed,” Della said. “The red tide became a killer.”

Harper asked, “What was the chemical you found?”

“Potassium,” Avery replied.

“Is that poisonous?”

“If you shoveled in enough of it, potassium could stop your system. But that isn’t the case here. Remember, people eat this seaweed all over the region.”

The third floor held two small classrooms, five labs, and seven offices. One lab was occupied by two female technicians, both bent over a laptop set on a central island. There was the muffled sound of a lone voice, talking through an office’s closed door. Otherwise the floor was empty. The hallway held the still hush of a summer lull. Cruz covered the floor in less than sixty seconds, gliding with the smooth speed of a ballroom dancer. He pushed through the exit at the front of the building and crossed the landing. The stairwell window overlooked the front entrance. He could see the hood of the target’s vehicle. Cruz faced three possibilities. There could be a basement lab behind the alarmed door, restricted because of their working with hazardous materials. He decided it was unlikely the university would allow a dangerous environment beneath three floors holding hundreds of people. Which meant either the target and his team were hidden behind one of the windowless office doors, or . . .

He slipped down the stairs and entered the second-floor hallway. He was in his element, a sleek predator cat moving soundlessly through the high grass. Hunting.

forty-two

"Phosphate isn't the killer. It isn't even the smoking gun."

Avery had said it four times before. Della did not mind. She actually liked the repetition. She took it to mean he was intensely engaged. So tightly focused that he was talking to himself out loud.

"Phosphate is like identifying a footprint at a murder scene. Our job is to find out how the footprint got there in the first place. Who made it. And lastly, *why*."

Each time Della signaled, Harper shifted to the next sequence. Della had lined them up according to Lanica's timeline. Each sequence started with the Lupa, the bloom. Then the algae growth turned a rich green, like an old-growth forest seen from above, only this one was underwater. And each time the fishing boats came out. Literally within hours of the bloom vanishing. Della was convinced Avery was right.

Theo stood back a couple of paces from Avery, giving the scientist space to roam. He said, "This was not the first season of Lupa. Not by a long shot."

Theo voiced what she had been thinking. Which Della liked. A lot. Being on the same wavelength, even on such a horrid topic, was still a kick.

Harper nodded. “The question we’ve got to answer is, what changed?”

“Something took this seaweed and turned it into a killing machine,” Della said. “But what?”

“Phosphate isn’t the reason,” Avery repeated, gliding around, almost dancing now, tapping the screen where the fishing boats plied their nets. “But it may lead us there.”

“Something tied to the phosphate,” Harper said.

“That’s my guess.” Avery stepped back, lifted his glasses, and rubbed his eyes. “What’s next?”

“Those are all the locations I’ve tapped into so far,” Della said.

“No, no, that’s enough. You’ve given the killer a face. It’s excellent work.”

Avery’s two lab techies had drifted in and were leaning against the windowsill at the back of the office. One of them clapped softly and said, “Bravo.”

Theo stepped forward. “Now it’s my turn.”

forty-three

Cruz was certain of his target's location the instant he pushed through the second floor's stairwell entrance. Two voices spoke from midway down the corridor and to his left. The walls were concrete and the floor shiny linoleum, with a typical drop ceiling and long fluorescent lights. The hallway served as a perfect baffle for the voices, one male and the other female. Then a third female voice spoke. Cruz had no idea if his target was one of those speaking. It did not matter. The sounds carried a high level of tension or excitement. All the voices were mature, older. Which meant they fit the group he had been tracking. He stood where he was, pretending to study a poster taped to the wall beside the exit. The entire second floor appeared to be empty, except for the two labs and the darkened room, which he now assumed held his target.

The problem was his location. The lab that opened into the darkened room was on the opposite side of his target. Cruz needed to have a look inside, make sure he was going after the right location. To be wrong meant he might be seen in attack mode by civilians. Which meant adding to the list of collateral damage. Worse, he might raise the alarm before the target went down.

Cruz went back through the exit and climbed the stairs, hitting every fourth step, adrenaline sparking everything he saw and touched and breathed. Halfway up the stairs, however, he was halted by a deafening *boom*.

Cruz froze on the middle landing and stared at the world beyond the stairwell window. His first thought was that the second set of shooters had found their target. But laughter followed, and he realized he'd been spooked by a steel exit door slamming against a concrete wall.

The other hunters loomed large in his mind. Cruz had survived this long by not taking chances. And by relying on his spider sense. Which was now telling him the second team was still out there. Watching.

As the voices receded, the silence was almost total. Cruz remained poised on the landing. Staring at the sunlight beyond the slit window. Checking the terrain. When he was certain, he continued up the stairs. Moving slower now. Cautious. Spooked by things he could not even define.

forty-four

Theo began, "Go back to what you said at the start."

Avery showed no irritation over being redirected. It was as tight a connection as Theo had known with the scientist. And this was good because Theo's gut told him they were on to something. The goal was not in sight. Not yet. But they were closing in. Maybe Avery and the two women knew this as well. He could sense the two of them moving a step closer. Leaving room for them to glance at the screen to Theo's left. Inspect the African waters clouded by the dark green mass.

"Track the peripheral evidence," Theo went on, "that's what you said, correct? What is your aim?"

Avery replied, "Seek a pattern. Use the pattern to formulate the right questions."

"Exactly." Theo pulled a whiteboard in close, erased Avery's scribbles, and wrote across the top, *Why was Kenny arrested?*

Theo turned around and liked what he found there in the three faces. Maybe they had become connected to the same energy that vibrated in his own gut. He thought he could detect that spark of excitement in their eyes.

Avery recalled, "That was the question Lanica told us to ask."

"Right. She said it would lead us to the hidden reality." Theo wrote another line, *Why was Kenny arrested NOW?*

"Opioids," Harper said.

Della shook her head. "No. There have been rumors swirling for over a year. It's how I got involved, assuming there was a hidden truth behind the tales. If someone had found a smoking gun, something definite, the headlines would shout it from every major newspaper."

Harper nodded slowly. "Makes sense."

"Timing," Theo said. "Timing is everything."

Avery frowned at the two new lines on the whiteboard. He opened his mouth but no sound emerged.

Theo took that as his cue and wrote a third line, *Who has the power to give the order?* He said, "Say it's not Africa at all. We've been assuming it's some regional power on the other side of the Atlantic. But my gut tells me we need to look closer to home."

"Don't forget the scary man at the airport," Della said.

"Right, okay. But how could an African ambassador have the clout to manipulate American federal agents? What if he was sent just to confuse the issue?" Theo gave that a beat, then wrote a fourth line, *What is the crisis issue?*

Harper said, "I have no idea what that means."

"Political economics," Theo said. "The point at which all subsequent events must be redefined."

"I like it," Harper decided.

"So do I," Della said.

Avery's eyes flashed from the whiteboard to the screen and back.

Theo said, "So the core question is, what could possibly be big enough that powerful forces with a global reach would feel the need to sweep hundreds of deaths under the carpet?"

Della stepped in close enough to brush against Theo. "And be able to keep their presence a secret."

Theo breathed in her scent and felt her closeness add to his sense of forces accumulating. He said to Harper, "Go back to that first bloom."

Harper brought the image back on-screen, bathing them in hues of red and danger. Theo stepped out of the light, drawing Della with him. Needing her closeness to fuel his thoughts. Or perhaps wanting it to be so. Which was enough just then. "Draw in tighter."

"We've already seen the boats," Avery protested from the screen's opposite side.

"Tighter still. Okay. Stop." The realization fired Theo with such force he felt incandescent. "Tell me what you see."

Avery shifted forward until his nose was scarcely a hand's breadth from the screen. "What are all those little dots?"

A simple nod of acknowledgment was not enough. Theo rocked his entire upper body. "Go to the next Lupa."

Della moved forward until her shadow was joined to Avery's. "There they are again."

"Will you two please step away from the screen so the rest of us can see it?" Harper did not wait for Theo's instruction. "Okay. Here's Lupa number three."

"More dots," Della said.

Harper asked, "Can you get any closer?"

"That's as tight as they allow," Della said. "You have to buy into a different feed, and that requires formal approval from one federal agency or another."

Avery said, "This isn't Google's photo view of your local neighborhood. These are conflict zones and contested regions."

"It's close enough," Theo said, and he marveled at how the thrill of discovery did not seem to touch his voice.

Della glanced over. "You know what they are?"

Theo nodded. "Ladies and gentlemen, I give you the smoking gun."

forty-five

Cruz entered the top floor and raced along the empty corridor to the hall's opposite end, then back down the second stairwell. He paused by the exit doorway long enough to ensure the Glock had a round in the chamber and the silencer was on tight. Then he pushed through the door.

As soon as Cruz exited the stairwell, he knew something had changed. The second-floor corridor had a breathless quality, like all the air had been sucked from the building. He padded silently to the lab. The two technicians were still there, hard at work, bent over their equipment. The late afternoon sun shone off their gloves and lab coats. One of them said something, the other laughed. The room adjacent to the lab with the waist-high glass partition was still dark. This time nothing flashed and there were no murmuring voices as Cruz approached the door. He opened it softly, and felt the air around him blister when he saw the room was empty.

Cruz realized he was no longer alone. He slipped the Glock back into his pack before stepping out of the room's shadows.

The woman was small and very dark. There was a singular intensity to her gaze and a bitter cast to her features. Cruz had the distinct impression she was not American, at least not by birth. He knew a number of recent immigrants who still carried the imprint of their past and whatever had forced them to leave their homeland. Bloodlines of such people were often much purer than those of most Americans. The woman's face was slanted by cheekbones that rose like twin mounds beneath almond-shaped eyes. She carried herself on her toes, like someone who had spent her entire life running. Cruz put her age at mid-twenties. Her dark hair was cropped short to her head, and her smile was slightly canted, as though the weight of her life pulled down one side. She wore tan shorts over muscular legs and running shoes with those little tab socks that left her ankles bare. She said, "How are you doing this fine day?"

"Could be better." He had no idea why he spoke at all. The woman had a honeyed accent he could not place. And the smile. It was very knowing, a magnetic draw that momentarily diminished his rage over the target's ability to keep just beyond range. "You?"

"Oh, this day just keeps getting finer." She moved past him with a dancer's lithe motions. "You stay cool now."

Cruz was tempted to follow her. But the day's course was set, and he had not the time for distractions, however magnetic. He kept to a calm pace until he reached the stairwell, and then he bounded down to the mid-floor landing.

Through the slit window, Cruz watched the target and the other man and one of the women climb into the Jeep. The dark-skinned attorney got into a second Cherokee. As she reversed out of the spot, she said something through her open window that caused Theo Bishop to smile.

Cruz felt the rage coalesce once more. He slapped the glass, then started down the stairs again. If they went straight back to the Fairview residence, Cruz would not be able to position himself in advance of their arrival. He could not rise from his carefully chosen lair. He had to take them all out. A frontal assault. The best he could hope for was that the kids were not home.

He left the building and ran for his car.

forty-six

Avery spent the entire journey back to Fairview talking through his next steps. Much of what he said made no sense to Theo. Perhaps if he had focused more intently, he could have followed the discussion better. But just then he was filled with a weary satisfaction. They had their target in sight.

"Numerous viruses infect plants," Avery said. "But very few of these infect humans. Only three, in fact. *Bunyaviridae*, *Rhabdoviridae*, and *Reoviridae*. Three out of thousands. The most common genus is the *Tobomovirus*. Highly stable and highly contagious. It requires no specific vector for transmission. But to my knowledge it has never been found in ocean vegetation."

Avery's voice carried a soft quality Theo had never heard before. He suspected Avery was not in fact speaking to them at all. Avery continued, "My guess is, we'll discover this outbreak is caused by a nanovirus, a genus not specifically tied to seaweed, which of course means it will be dismissed by many of my colleagues. But there are three reasons why I suspect they are wrong. Nanoviruses are extremely sensitive to pollutants. They can rapidly shift structure and adapt their DNA so as to feed off whatever nutrients are available. Secondly, nanoviruses exit the host plant by nuclear pore export and tubule-guided viral movement. Which means they could easily become airborne infections."

Avery was in the passenger seat, with Della seated directly behind him. She typed swiftly and looked up only to frown at the back of Avery's head. Avery tapped an index finger on his thigh in the tempo of his words. "The third reason why I suspect nanoviruses are our target is histocompatibility. There is a binding affinity of coat proteins that play an important role in the host immune and autoimmune systems. If pollutants have caused a mutation, granting the nanovirus the ability to cross species, they could carry this threat to humans."

Theo only half listened as the scientist droned on about how to identify the nanovirus and replicate the antibodies so that a vaccine might be created. The words formed a flowing backdrop as Theo worked through his own next steps. Then he realized Della was studying him in the rearview mirror. When he met her gaze, she said, "Is something troubling you?"

He liked how they were so in sync. The desire to tell her how he felt bubbled up inside him so intensely that Theo had to swallow to keep it down. He pulled up to the estate gates and lowered his window. "Does anybody remember the code?"

Both of his passengers looked askance. Della said, “The same as for all the doors.”

“Sorry, doesn’t help.”

“Two-three-seven-four-six,” Avery said. “How do you get into your apartment?”

“Simple.” Theo leaned out, punched in the numbers, then settled back behind the wheel as the gates swung open. “I never lock the door.”

“Is that wise?”

He accelerated up the graveled drive. “Probably not.”

Della leaned forward. “What’s the matter, Theo?”

He replied, “There is something we haven’t covered that might hold—”

Then he noticed the car.

forty-seven

His name had once been Barry. Nowadays he thought of the name as having belonged to a set of borrowed memories. Something left in a box by the roadside, just beyond the perimeter of a burned-out village. There had been a lot of those in his native Zambia. As a child he had often watched stragglers wander the roads leading out of fire-blackened townships, all their belongings piled on their heads or pulled behind them in carts. It would hardly have been a surprise to find a box of discarded memories lying there in the dust.

Barry's connection to his own past was just like that, blasted by heat and dust and emotions that blistered the brain. There had been so many uprisings to mar his childhood. The one that had killed his father did not even have a name.

His mother had left behind the farm that had been in her family for six generations and fled to South Africa. They had settled in a white township, in a hardscrabble cinder-block home with no running water and sporadic electricity. Barry had entered school with a silent, burning rage and a complete indifference to his own pain. He had fought when necessary and soon earned himself a reputation for being someone to avoid in battle.

An observant teacher had taken note of Barry's strength and his intelligence and his swift hands, and introduced him to a local boxing club. The club's owner had served with Barry's teacher in the armed forces under Botha, the disgraced leader of white South Africa. Both gentlemen maintained a close connection within the new army, renamed the South African National Defense Force. They brought in a mutual friend, a newly retired master sergeant, now serving as hunting guide to rich tourists. The three of them took Barry on a series of excursions deep into the African veld. Gradually the young man found himself able to reknit his world and develop a deep and abiding love for the continent's secret grandeur. By his eighteenth birthday, Barry was ready to claim a new destiny.

When it came time to sign his enlistment papers, he gave a different name. It was time to leave more than just his memories in the roadside dust.

Just as his three mentors had expected, Bruno sailed through basic training. He was then tapped to enter the South African Special Forces Brigade, colloquially known as the Recces. The Recces were South Africa's special ops unit. They were classed as the nation's counterinsurgency elite, specializing in long-range combat reconnaissance and airborne insertions. Bruno found a home there and would have stayed for life, but then a roadside device outside a Zimbabwean village ended all that and left him with seven bits of shrapnel embedded in his hips and spine.

His commanding officer offered Bruno an administrative gig, but he was not made for manning a desk. He took his pension and his medals and resigned his commission. Then he waited. Three weeks later, he received a different sort of enlistment offer. One that sent him out wherever and whenever the client said. The pay was far better, the medical care something else entirely. The group that arranged his contracts had doctors on staff who were specialists at solving problems like Bruno's. He would carry three of the shrapnel bits for the rest of his life. And his new gig had earned him four more wounds, one of them serious enough to have laid him out for three months. But Bruno walked upright and slept well and lived mostly without pain. It was far more than most people in his line of work could ever expect.

His current gig had started out as just another quick insertion and security operation. It really did not require someone of his skill set or level of experience. Yet the client was important enough and rich enough to demand the best. From the very outset, Bruno had the distinct impression that more was at work. This was confirmed when a new series of instructions arrived, ordering him to drop everything and fly with his crew to the United States. Where none of them had ever operated before. Even so, Bruno was assured he and the team would be met planeside by a man with enough authority to obtain them all visas. And weapons. If anything went wrong, or the man was not there to greet them, Bruno was ordered to sit tight, say nothing about who they were, and ask anyone within earshot for Martin Thorpe.

Soon as they hit the ground in Asheville, Bruno was convinced the threat was real and a hunter was out there. Someone so skilled that Bruno never actually spotted the hunter. But every good frontline soldier developed the ability to detect the unseen threat. It was what separated the survivors from those who did not make it home. And Bruno's spider sense told him that Theo had been right to ask for his help.

Knowing there was a valid threat was halfway to surviving the attack. Bruno kept himself on high alert and spread out his team, forming a loose and hidden net around Theo and his crew.

The instructors who had trained Bruno taught him all there was to know about operating in densely congested areas. The key to residential sweeps was keeping things fluid. Adapting constantly to the change of place, time, people, conditions. Bruno saw himself and his team as part of an unseen river, flowing silently in and out of spaces, finding the tight niches that most would miss, and doing so without losing a single second. His team's movements were blindingly fast and utterly silent.

Their goal was to bring the target in alive. With enough evidence to extract not a conviction, but a confession. Bruno had tried to tell the client this reduced their level of success. And failure meant bloodshed, he made that clear as well. But the client was insistent.

They stayed on high alert. Knowing that when the attack came, they would have only a very brief instant to keep things from going very bad indeed.

forty-eight

Cruz tracked the target's Jeep Cherokee from a position three cars back. He had come no closer because he was fairly certain where they were going. Plus, he could not risk having them notice him. The element of surprise was crucial to his attack. When the Fairview turnoff came into view, Cruz slowed further. He waited until they had passed through the stop sign at the top of the exit ramp. Then he hammered the gas pedal to the floor.

The rental vehicle's lousy engine sputtered, as if it were indignant that Cruz would punch it so hard. Then the motor slipped into overdrive and the car accelerated up the ramp. The local road was empty, but he halted at the stop sign and pretended to check carefully in both directions. The professor sped through a yellow light and took the next right, on the road home.

The pickup behind him beeped its horn. Cruz turned right and floored it again. He passed the flashing light and turned just as Bishop pulled up to the estate and lowered his window. Cruz watched as he turned away from the electronic control box and spoke to the passengers. Cruz clenched the wheel but otherwise he showed no response. Accelerating, he left the estate behind and was going almost eighty when he reached the next curve. He braked hard and spun the wheel. The car squealed its way through a 180-degree turn. Thankfully the road remained empty. As the car came out of the turn, Cruz jammed the gas pedal against the floor. The gates had just begun to close. Somehow he managed to squeak by with only an inch or so to spare on either side.

The target's vehicle was midway up the slope leading to the main house. Cruz felt his heart racing in time to the screaming engine.

forty-nine

The car came out of nowhere. Theo had difficulty believing it even existed. The gate was almost sealed shut. He could see the metal staves lining the entire drive. And yet here it was, a nondescript newish vehicle, either tan or gold or green, racing up the drive behind them.

Della was still leaning forward, asking, "What's the matter?"

He did it for her. Theo wasn't aware of the thinking process just then. He reacted instinctively. But when he thought about it later, his response and the thought were there in his brain, welded together with adrenaline and fear. He did it because Della was leaning forward, off center, and if the car hit them hard, it could hurt her badly.

He pressed the accelerator to the floor, jerked the steering wheel to the right, and aimed his Jeep off the drive and onto the lawn. Angled down.

The car *slammed* into his SUV, pushing him in the direction he was already going. The attack was no longer straight on, however. The angle was canted enough that it merely accelerated the Jeep's dive.

Theo kept the accelerator mashed to the floor, because the car was still there. Chasing them down the hill.

He bounced hard over a grassy ledge he had not even noticed until that very moment. The attacking vehicle was much lighter and catapulted up so high, Theo's glance in the rearview mirror revealed its underbody and four spinning wheels.

The car came down hard and kept coming. Theo carved a wide swath of raw earth from the manicured lawn. Straight ahead rose the closed front gates, the metal staves high and as sharp as fangs.

Behind him and from the left came three quick sounds, so close together they sounded almost like one. *Bang bang bang*.

Della screamed, *"Gun! Gun!"*

fifty

Cruz had the window down and his left hand extended all the way out, firing off three rounds. With the car's wild bounces over the grass, he did not expect to hit anything. The shots were intended to spook the driver and cause him to do something foolish.

Which he did.

The target jerked his vehicle farther to the right, angling back uphill. Away from the closed gates. If he had a remote control it would have been bad, at least for Cruz. They could have sped away and called the cops and the hit would have gone south. But they had coded into the drive and now they were trapped.

The uphill turn was a beginner's mistake. The Jeep Cherokee was a solid vehicle with a strong four-wheel-drive system and a short turning axis. But it was also big and top-heavy, not designed for high-speed turns. The SUV came around in a series of bouncy shudders, the engine screaming and the wheels spewing grass and dirt at Cruz's windshield. But the SUV's turn was too severe and the speed too high, and that was all that mattered. When Bishop's vehicle struck the stone ledge rimming the drive, Cruz saw two of its wheels rise up off the ground. The two remaining tires were slick from the mud and grass and damp still coating them. They threw out a barrage of white gravel, slowing the SUV's uphill progress almost to a halt.

Cruz slammed into the Jeep. He aimed for the girder sealing the frame between the two passenger doors. The assault came at the perfect moment. The SUV's wheels were at their highest point, almost like a metal beast showing its glistening belly in abject defeat.

The Jeep tilted farther. Cruz's own tires spun for traction. His engine howled in tandem to the Jeep.

The SUV tipped onto its side.

Through his open window, Cruz heard a woman's shrill scream.

The sound was oddly satisfying. As though all the disorder this job carried suddenly crystallized into one high-pitched note of sheer terror.

His door was jammed out of alignment by the two crashes. With a grunt, Cruz pushed against it with his shoulder, impatient to get down to the work at hand. Finally it opened with a metallic groan. He slid from the car, popped out the pistol's clip, fed in a fresh one, and rounded the SUV. The windshield was cracked and spackled, making it hard to identify his target. But Cruz could see the man shifting inside. For an instant he could not make out exactly what was happening and feared the target might be armed.

That was when he realized Bishop was shoving the man in the passenger seat into the back. Trying to protect him.

Cruz smiled as he raised his gun. The way people responded to the approach of death never ceased to amaze him.

Then he heard gunfire.

fifty-one

Theo's Jeep seemed to fall forever.

He sat there holding the wheel as they reached the critical point and tilted over. There was nothing he could do except regret. He knew he had done something terribly wrong, and it would probably get them all killed. He listened to the engine's grinding whir and realized his foot was still on the gas. For some reason he could not manage to lift his leg. Every muscle in his body was locked solid.

The force of the impact had knocked Della across the rear seat and silenced her scream. Until that moment she seemed capable of maintaining that high note forever without drawing another breath. Beside him, Avery groaned.

He heard the attacker's car door squeal open, followed by footsteps scrunching over the debris.

A man came into view. Theo thought he looked impossibly young. Almost a child. The man's image crept through the windshield's cracks and dirt. What Theo saw most clearly was the gun in his hand. It looked as big as a cannon.

The only thing he could think to do was release Avery's seat belt and let the man fall on him. Avery shouted with pain, or shock, or both. Theo ignored the scientist's protests and pushed him back through the opening between the seats, trying to get him into a position where Theo's body might possibly shield him.

It was a futile gesture. He knew this even as he kept pushing. But he had to do something.

Then he heard shots fired.

fifty-two

Cruz found it difficult to accept what he saw. The target was *so close*. He could *smell* the man, his fear, the nearness of his death. All there on the other side of that shattered glass.

But the threat was real and closing in. Three men clambered over the metal fence. They were shooting as they moved, but they were firing handguns and shooting uphill, and Cruz was almost completely shielded by the overturned SUV. They could see only the top of his head, which meant they were mostly firing to get his attention. He knew that, just as he knew he could easily take them. Still they kept firing. One of them, an older white man, gripped two of the staves just below the bladed tops and did a gymnast's move, heaving his body sideways, up and over the fence. He tumbled when he fell and came up with his gun out. Blasting away at the underbody of the SUV. Preventing Cruz from focusing on the target as they drew closer.

The two other men were much bigger, the largest man obsidian black, and both were having trouble cresting the fence. But they made it scarcely ten seconds behind the other.

Cruz slipped back alongside the passenger

door, where he was most protected and could still fire four clean shots. He took aim.

Like shooting ducks in a pond.

Then he realized someone was shooting from *behind.* Cruz spun around and recognized the small dark-skinned woman from the biology building. She moved impossibly fast. Pounding toward him, her boots *flying* over the gravel. Cruz raised his gun and was about to fire when her next shot took him high in the shoulder, spinning him around. He watched his own gun fly off into the grass. He needed to run after it, grab the weapon, and finish the job.

But just then he was forced to sit down.

Even before he struck the gravel, the woman landed on him. Or pounced. She was surprisingly strong. Her look, her snarling voice speaking a language he could not identify, let alone understand, the flash of her weapon as it came down on his head. So hard it knocked all the world to black.

fifty-three

Four nights later, Theo was awoken by a summer storm. The lightning crashed so close that the light and thunder arrived instantaneously. Theo had endured a number of nightmare flashes since the attack. Each had jolted him awake with violent intensity. Normally he saw the shooter raise his gun, the muzzle so huge it looked capable of swallowing him whole. The gunshot always woke him.

This morning was different.

Theo had always loved the predawn hour, ever since childhood when he and his father rose from their beds before the others and hiked the forested hills. Often the slopes were blanketed in a mist as soft as the early light. The feeling he carried today was almost as fine as those memories.

He and his team were all active and in sync. Together they raced farther and farther along their compass headings. They looked to him for leadership, even when he did not fully understand what they were doing. He still did not have all the answers, but the puzzle was fitting itself together. He trusted them to achieve whatever was necessary. What was more, they trusted him back.

Theo made coffee and stood in the pool house

doorway, watching the curtain of water spill off the eaves. They didn't need to leave for another hour and a half. He imagined the team up in the house, already busy with their days. Bruno had wanted to move Theo into the residence and cram his own crew in here. Theo pointed out that the idea was mildly ridiculous, four people stuffed into this studio apartment. He insisted Bruno take both the entire third floor and the vast empty garage for their guard work. Theo was becoming ever more comfortable with giving orders, and having them carried out.

The storm passed just twenty minutes later. Five minutes more and the sky cleared enough for the sun to cast a golden veil over the morning. Theo slipped into his trunks and goggles and dove into the pool. Avery's girls spent hours and hours in the water. Claudia called them her two noisy otters. Theo loved their company and the simple joy they found in almost every minute of the day. He had taken to swimming before they came down, stroking from end to end, reveling in the crisp morning air and the sunlit ripples.

Only this morning was different.

When the shadow appeared above the pool's far end, Theo assumed it was one of Bruno's team. They were on constant patrol twenty-four seven and gave him some fairly mild heat for remaining on his own. But Theo liked the space, liked the hours he could spend here alone, working through next steps and coming to terms with the new direction his life was taking.

Only today it was not a guard.

Della gasped as she lowered herself slowly down the ladder. “It’s freezing.”

“It’s also easier if you just jump in and get it over with.”

“Is that any way to greet a lady?”

“Probably not.” He stripped off his goggles and set them on the pool’s edge. “Good morning.”

“That was some storm.” She released the ladder and reached for his arm. “Swim for me.”

He started backstroking toward the shallow end. “The idea is to get exercise for yourself.”

“You old romantic, you.” She kissed him. They had been close like this ever since the evening after the attack. The shootout, followed by four hours spent at the police station, had rendered them both too strung out and exhausted to hold back their feelings any longer. Still, they were constantly surrounded by people and urgent work. Which meant her kisses remained very rare and very special. Theo shivered at the warm-cold taste of her lips.

Della let go of him. “See, you’re cold too.” She stroked over to the shallow end and climbed the stairs out of the water. She knew he was watching her and smiled back down at him. “Claudia says you’re coming for breakfast in ten minutes or else she’ll send the girls down to fetch you.”

Theo did not move until she had climbed the ridge and disappeared into the house. She was lithe as a dancer, the muscles along her back and legs clearly defined. Theo knew she had run track and hurdles through college. They had run together twice at sunset, the female guard from Guinea-Bissau tracking them the entire time. Theo loved how Della had slowed her pace so as not to show them up.

Breakfast was served at the long counter, everyone talking loudly to be heard over the two chattering girls. Their energy was astonishing. As was Claudia's ability to handle them with such calm ease. Theo had twice phoned Amelia and invited her to join them. She had thanked him and declined, but had agreed to bring the kids over for a swim. Theo did not consider it a wise move, Amelia staying on her own, not with the risks being so real, and no matter how good her security detail might be. But he did not press the issue.

They planned while they ate. Later, Harper drew him aside to discuss several important items on her list. She had effectively taken over the running of their newly revived company. Preston Borders, the Washington attorney, was helping them in remarkable ways. His firm's investigators had unearthed evidence of collusion between the competitors who had driven Theo's company to the brink of bankruptcy. Together, Preston and Harper had filed suit in federal court, suing their opponents for fifty million dollars. Harper expected to settle within a matter of weeks.

But this wasn't what sparked the morning with an excitement that dwarfed the predawn storm. No one spoke about it, because there was nothing to be said really. The evidence of what was about to come shone from every face.

Ninety minutes later, they left the compound in two rented Chevy Tahoes. Bruno drove them in the second vehicle, while the first was driven by Henri. They traveled in a convoy everywhere now. Theo did not like it but saw no point in complaining. The others followed his lead.

The lower lawn remained gouged and torn, the graveled drive a mess. But the overturned vehicle and the bullet casings were all gone. Even so, Theo could still smell the burnt cordite. He thought the memory formed a worthy spice for what was about to happen.

When they arrived at the Asheville airport, a third Tahoe was pulled up next to the private air terminal. Amelia and two guards emerged and followed Theo and his team toward the jet stationed closest to the entrance. Bruno and Simone, the dark-skinned woman, accompanied them. They did not speak as the jet's engines whirred to life and they took off. Amelia did not look good. She sat hunched in the single seat next to the galley, her features tight and shadowed by exhaustion. Theo had been speaking to her every day since the attack, filling her in on developments. The whole ordeal had distressed her terribly. Not so much because Theo had been in danger, but rather because of what it might mean for Kenneth. Theo's brother was in solitary confinement inside a federal pen. Which was about as safe as anyone could be within the penal system. Theo found a great deal of comfort in that assurance. But Amelia clearly did not share his satisfaction.

Theo asked Amelia if she wanted a coffee. When she did not respond, he poured one for himself and slipped into the seat opposite her. Della had saved him a seat on the plane's opposite side. He would rather be there. But this needed to be done.

Theo said, "We're hoping Kenny will be released this afternoon."

Amelia turned from her blind inspection of the clouds and the light. "For real?"

"Tomorrow at the latest. At least that's what Preston is saying."

"Why am I hearing this from you and not Preston?"

"My guess is, Kenny didn't want to get your hopes up. We only heard on the way to the airport." Theo sipped his coffee and said the words that had compelled him to come and sit with her. "I owe Kenny a great debt."

Amelia resumed her inspection of the world beyond her window.

"I know you think this is somehow your fault. If you hadn't drawn Kenny into your faith, none of it would have happened."

"I should have known," she said to the window. "He's so intense about everything. So *total.* I should have seen this coming. It's like pouring gasoline on an open flame. I should have—"

"Amelia, you did the right thing. The Kenny I grew up with was . . ." Theo paused and took another drink of his coffee, searching for the right words. "Brutally competitive. I sometimes wondered what appealed to him the most—winning, or seeing his opponents in the dust."

She did not give any indication she heard him at all.

Theo went on, "He probably was involved in the opioid overdose crisis. That's most likely what you rescued him from. You need to remember that whenever—"

"Stop," she whispered.

Even so, he continued, "When Kenny came to see me, I knew instantly I was dealing with a different man. He was right to tell you not to explain when I asked. I needed to witness it from the inside. And accept the invitation behind his silence."

A single tear trickled down her cheek. It was the only response Theo needed to know he had been right to speak. "Kenny isn't just a different man, Amelia. He's a *better* man. He *challenges* me."

Amelia wiped her cheeks with a shaky hand. When it settled back on the table between them, Theo reached over and gripped it. Her fingers were wet from her tears. Theo said, "I'm a better man because of your husband and who he has become. And something more. I'm glad he reached out to me. Despite everything. So very, very grateful."

Amelia nodded. "I love him so much."

"I know you do," Theo said. "And now he deserves your love."

fifty-four

They landed forty-five minutes later at a private airstrip in Prince George County, Virginia. A pair of Cadillac Escalades was there to greet them. Standing beside the front vehicle was the man Theo had last seen in the windowless bowels of Dulles Airport. Martin Thorpe wore another blazer, this one slate gray with narrow black stripes, black trousers, white shirt, and black silk tie with silver dashes. He stepped forward as Theo reached the tarmac. "Good to see you again." He shook Theo's hand and added, "Good to see you alive."

"Thanks again for getting Bruno's team in place."

"Happy to help." He turned to Amelia. "Martin Thorpe, Ms. Bishop. I'm hoping this is the last time you'll need to visit your husband in a place like this."

Amelia seemed reluctant to take his hand. "And you are?"

"A friend," Theo said. "Martin is why this meeting is taking place at all."

"Me and a number of allies," Martin added. "Speaking of which, we have some powerful people waiting on us. Best if we get this show on the road."

But Amelia did not budge. "Kenny warned me not to trust anyone who claimed to be my friend."

"Those times are behind you," Martin replied.

Amelia crossed her arms. "In case you hadn't noticed, whoever you are, my husband is still in jail."

Theo stepped in between them. "Martin is with Homeland Security. He came to see me when we were halted at Dulles. My guess is, Martin represents the minority voice within US intelligence."

Amelia's grip on her forearms tightened. "Which means what exactly?"

When Theo looked at Martin, the agent shook his head. "It's better if you spell it out."

"Being held at the airport was actually a good thing," Theo said. "It brought home the fact that Kenny's warnings weren't just meant for while we were in Africa. The OAS ambassador might as well have shouted it in my ear. If they could, they were going to shut us down."

By this point, all the others had moved in around them. Della said, "We sort of knew that already."

"Right. But that was the moment when the threat became something we had to face. And deal with. So after we were released, I called Martin and asked him to help put Bruno and his team in place."

"Secretly," Martin said. "I liked that part. And so did my superiors. They liked it a lot."

"Explain that," Avery said. "On account of the secrecy and the guy attacking us . . . what was his name?"

"Cruz," Della said. "And the answer is, evidence."

"Kenny wouldn't tell me who was behind the threats," Theo said. "But I think he suspected all along that it wasn't any African country or the OAS."

Martin offered a smile that did not touch his eyes. "They colluded. They did not direct."

Theo nodded. "They had some secret ally closer to home, somebody who was the *real* threat, and powerful enough to put Kenny in jail and stifle his chances of raising the alarm."

"And the only chance we had of identifying them was by doing as Theo suggested," Martin said. "Putting your team out there in plain view. Letting you get on with your work. Showing these people that Kenny was not the only one looking to connect the dots."

"And having Bruno secretly in place to protect us," Theo added.

Della looked from one to the other. "So . . . we were used as bait?"

Avery's squint was almost as tight as Amelia's. "You never expected us to identify what or who was behind the outbreak, did you?"

"That was definitely icing on the cake." Martin glanced at his watch. "Folks, this has been fun, but we're late to the dance. Let's go get Kenny out of jail."

Thirty-five minutes later, they pulled into the parking lot fronting the Federal Correctional Institution of Petersburg. The main building could have belonged to a corporate headquarters or a school. The whitewashed structure was surrounded by a carefully groomed lawn and flags flapping in the hot summer wind. It was only when Theo approached the side entrance that he could see the fencing and the razor wire and the guard towers.

A guard stationed inside the doorway asked for their IDs. They were processed through, then their security detail were ordered to wait for them in the lobby. A uniformed officer then led them through the bulletproof inner door.

They were ushered upstairs and into a conference room that already held three men and a stern-looking gray-haired woman, who greeted them with, "I've been cooling my heels here for half an hour, Martin. I dislike time wasters."

"Emily Crouch," Martin said. "Deputy US attorney general. This is Dr. Theo Bishop and his team, the group I've been telling you about."

She dismissed them with a single dark look. "Let's get this under way."

Martin gestured them into seats without

introducing the dark-suited men. Theo saw no need to ask about their identities. Their taut builds and uniformly blank expressions and cautious gazes said it all.

Amelia asked, "Where's Kenny?"

"Coming." Martin slipped into a chair between the woman and the three dark suits. "Emily, do you mind getting us started?"

She turned to Theo. "Dr. Bishop, how certain are you of this being a genuine and deadly outbreak?"

"A hundred and ten percent."

"There is no room for doubt?"

"None."

"Can you offer us any hard evidence?"

"Absolutely," Theo said.

"I'm not talking about some attack in a remote village nine thousand miles from here. One that doesn't officially exist anymore."

Theo did not mind her cold analytical nature in the least. "All we need is one hurricane to carry the Lupa virus across the Atlantic, and you'll have all the evidence you could ask for. Dumped right here on your doorstep."

"And I'll make it my business to inform the world that you were given fair warning of it," Della added.

Emily Crouch's gaze did not waver until the side door opened and Preston Borders walked in, followed by Kenny.

If anything, Theo's brother had lost more weight. He accepted Amelia's embrace and looked over the top of her head to ask Theo, "Do you have it?"

"We're closing in." Theo gestured to Avery. "He and his team have been working around the clock."

Kenny released Amelia and asked Avery, "How long do you need?"

"A month, six weeks tops. We've isolated the nanovirus."

"Make it less."

Avery did not object. "We'll try."

"Whatever you need," Kenny said. Then he looked down at his wife and smiled for the first time that Theo could recall since all this started.

Emily shifted impatiently. "Let's get back on target. Tell me what you have."

fifty-five

Avery showed no interest in addressing the AG, so Theo served as the team's spokesman. He kept waiting for Avery or Della to chime in, correct him, say he'd gotten something totally wrong. But they remained silent, probably preferring his errors to making themselves targets of Emily Crouch's darkly burning expression.

It had all come down to starting with the right questions.

Which led to answering the mysteries they had scrawled across the whiteboards.

Phosphate in the blood.

They could then view the drilling rigs seen near all the Lupa outbreaks for what they were.

All drilling stations, whether on land or in shallow waters or even on massive deepwater rigs, had one thing in common.

They used mud.

Tons and tons of mud. It was pumped through the piping, known as the drill string, down to where it sprayed through nozzles on the drill bit. This both cleaned and cooled the bit as it spun.

The mud was then pushed back up the drilled hole, the annular space, carrying with it fragments of crushed rock known as cuttings. Once this compound emerged from the surface casing, it was filtered through a shale shaker, and the mud returned to the pit to be reused.

Chemicals were constantly being added to the mud pit, mostly lubricants. But one compound in particular was used by the ton.

Potassium.

Clays and chemicals were added to water in the mud pit, creating a homogenous blend that resembled a milk shake. The most common clay additive was bentonite, called "gel" in the oil business. The mud maintained a constant fluid state, even under the extreme conditions at the drill head, through the bentonite and potassium it contained.

The largest source of bentonite clay was to be found in Fort Benton, Wyoming, where numerous volcanoes provided constant replenishment of the local clay pits. The first thing Avery did upon identifying the rigs as a potential source of the trouble was to obtain samples and grow his own lab samples of *ecklona maxima*, the most common version of African seaweed.

None of these sources produced a nanoviral shift that might indicate a move toward a red tide, a bloom, or a threat.

Which was when Avery proved himself a true scientist.

He went looking for another source of bentonite.

It was through Bruno's contacts that he found

one. And obtained samples that the company still didn't know had been taken.

Six hundred kilometers inland from the West African coast, a clutch of hot springs spewed a noxious blend of clay and sulphur.

Recent satellite footage showed that the entire region had been fenced off. Guard towers erected. Massive earthmoving equipment brought in. Trucks and new roads and workers' compounds also erected.

There was no way Theo's team could ever officially obtain a sample from this region. Soldiers and private security patrolled inside the compound and beyond the perimeter fence.

But Bruno arranged for the samples to be stolen and flown straight to Avery's lab.

Nineteen hours later, the first toxic nanoviruses were detected.

Emily Crouch demanded, "Do you know who owns the mine?"

Martin slid over a sheet of paper. "An Indonesian company with close ties to the central government."

She aimed her gun-barrel gaze down at the page. "Who are their customers?"

Martin Thorpe gave his easy smile. "That's where things get interesting."

New developments in geological soundings had revealed more oil in the shallow waters off the

African Atlantic coastline than in all the Middle Eastern countries combined. Access was fairly easy. Drilling technologies were well used to working in waters of such depths.

The problem was access. As in, these waters were controlled by countries whose governments demanded bribes.

Bribing government officials was against the law in most western nations. Even when billions of barrels were at stake.

Which was where the Indonesian oil companies came in. The problem was, Indonesia's oil companies were not specialists in offshore drilling. So they went looking for a partner.

None of the majors would dare touch such a project, not with the current political conditions. There was too much risk of their being tainted by Indonesian business practices. So the Indonesians found a smaller group. A family-owned company specializing in high-risk offshore projects. Billings Oil, out of Houston.

Emily Crouch heard them out in silence, tapped her pen on the table a few times, then said, "What I've heard so far is very interesting, but it doesn't come close to giving us anything that would stand up in a court of law. We need *hard evidence*. A smoking gun that would tie Billings Oil directly to an act that is illegal under American law."

Martin Thorpe's grin grew larger still. "Now things get really interesting." He slid over a second sheet of paper.

"What's this?"

"Call log from the shooter's phone. Those seven numbers highlighted in yellow? They can be traced back to an investigator in Texas. This guy has just one client. A law firm. Guess who that law firm's biggest client is?"

One of the dark suits leaned back in his chair, tilted his head toward the ceiling, and said, "Bingo."

Preston Borders spoke for the first time since entering the room. "I would say this nullifies any reason your office has for holding my client. Wouldn't you agree?"

Emily Crouch shook her head without taking her eyes off the highlighted sheet. "There's still the issue of Mr. Bishop's involvement in the opioid crisis."

"No, there isn't," Martin Thorpe replied. "Not today."

"Excuse me?"

Martin pointed an index finger skyward. "Orders from the very tip-top."

Preston went on, "My client's team has just supplied you with solid gold evidence. Not to mention Bishop Pharma being involved in the urgent development of a vaccine to stop Lupa from invading our coastal regions."

“The man has a point,” Martin said. “Two of them, in fact.”

Preston rose to his feet. “Sign his release, Ms. Crouch. Let my client get back to saving millions of lives.”

Theo added, “While there’s still time.”

fifty-six

Preston Borders flew back to Asheville with them so he and Harper could plan their legal assault on the collective that had bankrupted their firm. Marilyn Riles, the associate who had rescued them from the Dulles lockup, accompanied them as well. She and Preston showed an almost gleeful excitement over the upcoming arbitration and settlement hearing.

Kenny spent the flight holding his wife's hand. It was only now, when they were seated together at thirty thousand feet, that Theo could see the similarity to their expressions. Both of them looked far beyond any measure of normal exhaustion.

At Kenny's request, Preston and Harper and Marilyn took their discussion of battle tactics farther toward the nose of the aircraft. Della and Avery slipped into the chairs opposite theirs while Theo seated himself across the aisle. Amelia looked his way and smiled slightly. The tight compression to her lips was easing. Theo took that as a good sign.

Kenny asked Avery, "Any indication of a hurricane?"

"There are three possible depressions strung out from the African coast," Avery replied. "The third one shows the greatest risk of becoming a major storm."

"Any word on its path?"

Della answered, "We're talking daily with the experts. They say it's much too early to give any valid prediction. But the greatest likelihood is landfall in the Lesser Antilles."

"When?"

"Fourteen, maybe fifteen days."

"Avery?"

"We're working on it twenty-four seven."

Theo said, "Martin Thorpe has been a huge help. He's opened doors at the NIH, FDA, CDC. But the most valuable of all has been the National Institute of Allergy and Infectious Diseases. They're new, they're flexible, and they get it. Whatever we need, they make happen in a matter of hours."

"And they have gotten us some material I haven't even managed to think about yet," Avery confessed.

Kenny nodded. "And Martin is . . . ?"

"Homeland Security, is all I know. Has to be high up, to get things moving like he has."

Preston called over, "The African States ambassador who confronted you at Dulles has been recalled. I detect our Mr. Thorpe is hard at work."

Theo added, "And he got Dr. Lanica out. She didn't want to come, of course. But Martin thought she'd be much safer teaching a refresher course in pediatric surgery in Chicago. Let things settle down. Once the crisis goes public, she's in the clear. And Martin assures us there are two good replacement doctors serving as her locum."

"Two doctors won't be enough to cover her load," Della said.

Theo thought Kenny wanted to smile at their easy banter, yet his face seemed incapable of recalling how to reform itself.

Amelia turned to her husband. "You're going down, aren't you?"

"Down where?"

"Don't give me that. You know perfectly well what I mean."

"The Antilles." Kenny nodded. "I need to be there."

"No, you don't. Not really. But you're going. It's who you are. And I'm going with you."

"Amelia . . ." Whatever else Kenny was about to say became stifled by the look she gave him. It was a fractional change, just a slight tilt to her face, a little jut to her chin, a bit of steel to her gaze. Enough to make Kenny sigh and ask, "What about the kids?"

"They're coming with us. What do you think?"

"Amelia, this could be dangerous. The vaccine will be completely untested."

"Save it. You're going, I'm going. The kids have heard for weeks that Daddy is working so hard and he's even gone to prison to save the islands from getting sick. They need to see you in action to make it all real."

"But—"

"They need this, Kenny. And so do I."

Theo said, "I want to go too."

Della said, "I'm coming. Absolutely."

Kenny looked from one face to the other. And for a brief instant the dark tension that had carried him through so much just melted away. He cleared his throat, looked at his wife, and said, "I wouldn't have it any other way."

Davis Bunn is an award-winning novelist and Writer-in-Residence at Regent's Park College, University of Oxford. His books, published in twenty-five languages, have sold over eight million copies worldwide. After completing degrees in international economics and finance in the United States and England, Davis became a business executive working in Europe, Africa, and the Middle East. He draws on this international experience in crafting his stories. Davis has won four Christy Awards for excellence in historical and suspense fiction and was inducted into the Christy Hall of Fame. He and his wife, Isabella, divide their time between the English countryside and the coast of Florida. To learn more, visit DavisBunnBooks.com.